THE PENGUIN CLASSICS

Founder Editor (1944–64): E. V. Rieu

Ivan Sergeyevich Turgenev was born in 1818 in the Province of Orel, and suffered during his childhood from a tyrannical mother. After the family had moved to Moscow in 1827 he entered Petersburg University where he studied philosophy. When he was nineteen he published his first poems and, convinced that Europe contained the source of real knowledge, went to the University of Berlin. After two years he returned to Russia and took his degree at the University of Moscow. In 1843 he fell in love with Pauline Garcia-Viardot, a young Spanish singer, who influenced the rest of his life, he followed her on her singing tours in Europe and spent long periods in the French house of herself and her husband, both of whom accepted him as a family friend. He sent his daughter by a sempstress to be brought up among the Viardot children. After 1856 he lived mostly abroad, and he became the first Russian writer to gain a wide reputation in Europe; he was a well-known figure in Parisian literary circles, where his friends included Flaubert and the Goncourt brothers, and an honorary degree was conferred on him at Oxford. His series of six novels reflect a period of Russian life from the 1830s to the 1870s: they are *Rudin* (1855), *A House of Gentlefolk* (1858), *On the Eve* (1859, a Penguin Classic), *Fathers and Sons* (1862), *Smoke* (1867) and *Virgin Soil* (1876). He also wrote plays, which include the comedy *A Month in the Country*; short stories and *Sketches from a Hunter's Album* (a Penguin Classic); and literary essays and memoirs. He died in Paris in 1883 after being ill for a year, and was buried in Russia.

Sir Isaiah Berlin, who was President of the British Academy from 1974 until 1978, is a Fellow of All Souls College, Oxford, and an Honorary Fellow of Corpus Christi College, Oxford. He has received honorary doctorates from the Universities of Columbia, Cambridge, London, Jerusalem and Tel Aviv, among others. His published work includes some notable contributions to Russian studies. He has written *The Hedgehog and the Fox*, an essay on Tolstoy's view of history, and several essays on Alexander Herzen, and he gave the Romanes Lecture on Turgenev's *Fathers and Children*, included in the Penguin Classics translation of the same work (under the title *Fathers and Sons*). He has also translated Turgenev's *First Love* for the Penguin Classics. His superb translation of *A Month in the Country* was specially commissioned by the National Theatre. He is also the author of several books on political theory. In 1979 he was awarded the Jerusalem Prize for his writings on the freedom of the individual in society.

МЕСЯЦ
В ДЕРЕВНЕ

ИВАН
ТУРГЕНЕВ

A MONTH
IN THE COUNTRY

A Comedy in Five Acts

by Ivan Turgenev

Translated and Introduced
by Isaiah Berlin

PENGUIN BOOKS

Penguin Books Ltd, Harmondsworth, Middlesex, England
Penguin Books, 40 West 23rd Street, New York, New York 10010, U.S.A.
Penguin Books Australia Ltd, Ringwood, Victoria, Australia
Penguin Books Canada Ltd, 2801 John Street, Markham, Ontario, Canada L3R 1B4
Penguin Books (N.Z.) Ltd, 182–190 Wairau Road, Auckland 10, New Zealand

First published in Great Britain by the Hogarth Press 1981
First published in Canada by Clarke, Irwin & Co. Ltd 1981
First published in the United States of America by The Viking Press 1982
Published in Penguin Books 1983

Translation, Introductory Note and Appendix
Copyright © Isaiah Berlin, 1981
All rights reserved

Printed and bound in Great Britain by
Cox & Wyman Ltd, Reading
Set in Garamond

All applications for professional and amateur performing rights
in this translation of the play should be addressed to
Spokesmen, 1 Craven Hill, London W2 3EP

CONTENTS

The first production of this new translation of *A Month in the Country* opened at The Olivier Theatre, South Bank, London, on 19 February 1981. The cast was as follows:

ARKADI SERGEYEVICH ISLAYEV, Robert Swann
NATALAYA PETROVNA, Francesca Annis
KOLYA, Alex Paterson / Jake Rea
VERA ALEKSANDROVNA, Caroline Langrishe
ANNA SEMYONOVNA ISLAYEVA, Betty Hardy
LIZAVETA BOGDANOVNA, Mary Macleod
ADAM IVANOVICH SCHAAF, Leonard Fenton
MIKHAILO ALEKSANDROVICH RAKITIN, Nigel Terry
ALEKSEI NIKOLAYEVICH BELYAEVW, Ewan Stewart
AFANASI IVANOVICH BOLSHINTSOV, David Ryall
IGNATI ILYICH SHPIGELSKY, Michael Gough
MATVEI, Ron Pember
KATYA, Holly de Jong

with Paul Bentall, Paul Bradley, Clare Byam Shaw, Susan Porrett, John Rees, Kate Saunders, Peter Sproule, Di Trevis, David Troughton.

Designer: Alison Chitty; music by George Fenton.
The production was directed by Peter Gill.

INTRODUCTORY NOTE

A Month in the Country is Turgenev's seventh play. He wrote it
while living in Paris during the revolutionary years 1848–50, when
the influence upon him of his radical friends, Belinsky and Herzen,
was strongest, the years during which he began the composition of
A Sportsman's Sketches which first made him famous both as a writer
and as a champion of the oppressed. The play was intended for
publication in *The Contemporary*, a liberal Petersburg periodical
edited by his friends, the poet Nekrasov and the critic Panaev; the
completed text reached them in 1850. The play was originally
called *The Student*, and after that *Two Women*. There has been
some dispute among Russian critics in this century about the degree
to which Turgenev might have been influenced in writing this play
by Balzac's *La marâtre* ('The Step-mother'), which its author insisted on describing as a drawing-room comedy. It appeared, with
considerable success, on the Paris stage in 1848, when Turgenev
might well have seen it. There are certainly striking similarities
between these 'comedies': *La marâtre* is also concerned with the
love of a young woman and of her much younger step-daughter (or
ward) for a young man employed in their service. Here, too, the
older woman tries to get rid of her young ward by marrying her off
to a dried-up old man, and, in addition, the plot includes a cunning,
cynical doctor, at once an intriguer and an ironical observer. These
parallels can scarcely be accidental. Yet the entire atmosphere and
tone and moral centre of Turgenev's play are wholly different from
those of Balzac's drama, if only because of the central role of the
pathetic lover, Rakitin. By his own admission, Turgenev identified
himself with Rakitin, as he did in all his frequent portrayals of
unsuccessful lovers – he tended towards this kind of conscious
self-caricature all his life. Moreover, he placed his personages in the
environment that he knew best, a country house inhabited by
minor Russian gentry in a distant province – a society, an outlook,
and a way of life very different from the world of Balzac and the
West. In 1850 the play was submitted to the Russian censors who
demanded some major changes, including the transformation of
Natalya Petrovna into a widow (and the consequent elimination of
her husband Islayev and the transference of some of his lines to his

mother, who was permitted to survive), presumably because the love of a married woman for a man other than her husband could not be portrayed on the Russian stage. Turgenev complained, but, although he appeared to be ready to make all the required changes, permission to stage *Two Women* was finally refused. The play, by this time renamed *A Month in the Country*, first saw the light in *The Contemporary* in 1855, with the omissions and changes originally demanded by the censors.* The editors' plan to issue it a year later in a separate edition miscarried. It next appeared, with various minor corrections and additions made by the author, in the edition of his collected works published in 1869. Turgenev seems to have made no effort to restore the cuts made by the censors, save for at least one significant passage.* He held no high opinion of this or any other of his plays. 'This is not really a comedy,' he wrote in 1854 in a preface to the unpublished edition, 'but a novel in dramatic form. It will not do for the stage – that is clear. The kind readers must judge whether it will do in its published form.' Most Russian dramatic critics in the nineteenth century accepted this verdict and paid relatively little attention to the play.

A *Month in the Country* was first acted in Moscow on 13 January 1872, with cuts* only too easily agreed to by the author, who warned the principal actress that in his opinion the play was not worth performing, the public would find it much too tedious. The performance made little impression on the critics or the public. Turgenev, perhaps the least vain of famous authors, suffered throughout his life from a singular lack of confidence in his own literary ability, and constantly sought advice and criticism from his friends, which he almost invariably accepted. He therefore showed no surprise at this failure. The famous critic Druzhinin had told him in an article that he was no dramatist; this merely confirmed it.

Seven years later a well-known young actress, Maria Gavrilovna Savina, attracted by the part of Vera, chose the play for a special, so-called 'benefit', performance for herself, and acted in it in St Petersburg in January 1879. She asked the author for permission to make the inevitable cuts (the uncut version could take something over five hours). He sent her his usual discouraging message, advising her not to appear in it since it was unworthy of her gifts (of which, as she later remarked, he can have known nothing). The

* See Appendix: 'The Censorship of the Text', p. 124.

performance was a triumphant success. Turgenev returned to St Petersburg from France in early February; it took him more than a month to bring himself to see his play. Savina, with some difficulty, obtained permission to place the Director's box at his disposal. Although he tried to conceal himself behind a curtain, he was recognised and received a tremendous ovation. Savina tugged at his sleeve, but nothing would induce him to appear with the actors on the stage – he was not a playwright, it would not be appropriate. Savina's performance moved him very deeply. He told her that she *was* Verochka, that he had never imagined that this part could be so acted; he had not thought much about Verochka, Natalya Petrovna was the centre of his attention. So, too, when he found in a later performance by another company, that the part of Bolshintsov was marvellously acted, he said that he had never expected, never dreamt, that so much could be made of Bolshintsov, else he would have provided more material for it. Turgenev was over sixty when he met Savina; she was thirty. He found her irresistibly attractive, and remained in love with her for the rest of his days (he died four years later, in 1883). Their relationship was almost certainly purely platonic. She was at once delighted and embarrassed by the strength of his feeling; and he – the unsurpassed painter of unhappy love, of love as servitude, a theme which was never wholly absent from his writings, from *The Diary of a Superfluous Man* and *A Correspondence*, to *Torrents of Spring, Asya, Fathers and Sons, Virgin Soil* – wrote her letters, sentimental, ironical, self-mocking, the letters of a frustrated, ageing lover. Savina's performance made the play famous. It gradually entered the theatrical repertoire in every part of the world, and became one of the most admired and frequently acted nineteenth-century plays. Chekhov's *Seagull* and *Uncle Vanya* are its best known direct descendants.

The play was performed in the Moscow Art Theatre in 1909, directed by Stanislavsky and Moskvin. Stanislavsky played the part of Rakitin, and Chekhov's widow, Olga Knipper, acted Natalya Petrovna. In his memoirs and letters* Stanislavsky has

---

* K. S. Stanislavsky, *Sobraniye sochineniy v vos'mi tomakh*, Moscow, 1954, t.l. (translated as *My Life in Art*), pp. 297–306, 326–32; t.7 (letters 337–9 to N. V. Driesen, N. A. Popov and Olga Knipper-Chekhova), pp. 451–4. *See also* B. M. Sushkevich and O. L. Knipper-Chekhova, *O Stanislavskom, Sbornik vospominaniy*, Moscow, 1948, pp. 264–5, 380–1.

many interesting things to say about his production. His friend and colleague, Nemirovich-Danchenko, had earlier seen the play primarily as an evocation of an older Russia, an epoch and a society in which Turgenev was born and bred, 'flesh of its flesh, blood of its blood', an expression of 'its entire material and spiritual life'. For Stanislavsky it was a timeless, psychological study of the fine, perpetually altering nuances, the scarcely perceptible oscillations of the vicissitudes of passionate feeling, reflected in dialogue of exquisite sensibility, and the most authentic imaginable rendering of the interplay of emotions – the jealousies, sufferings, confusions of feeling, the waxing and waning of the loves and hatreds of the protagonists. He saw it as a web of delicate, unanalysable patterns – the lace-making in an airless room of Natalya Petrovna's simile – which the actors, in his view, could not begin to convey by means of the usual 'gestures, movements of hands and feet', but only by conveying an 'inner image', impalpable 'expressions of feeling and volition, by means of a look', a mere, hardly noticeable, inflexion of the voice; this, said Stanislavsky, was the only means of achieving 'an inner delineation of character'. In letters written a month before the performance, he said: 'There will be no *mise en scène*. A bench, a sofa, where people arrive, sit, talk – no sounds, no details . . . everything is based on what is experienced, on intonations. The entire play is woven out of the sensations and feelings of the author and the actors . . . The play is so psychologically fine that it doesn't allow of any décor,' scarcely any gestures. He tried to convey this to the principal actress, Olga Knipper. During one of the early rehearsals she burst into tears and said that she could not go on: the play was too motionless, too monochrome – that, at least, is what one gathers from her memoirs and letters. She left the theatre and went home in a state of near despair. Stanislavsky wrote her a famous letter in which he tried to express his understanding of her condition and his profound sympathy with it. She was grateful and comforted. When she finally returned, he explained to her that in his view the play was best acted in sections, that is, without necessary continuity either of mood or tone. Natalya Petrovna is a 'hot-house plant who wants to be a field flower – she dreams of meadows, woods . . . simple, natural life . . . hence Belyaev'. She bullies Vera, she 'scares her out of her simple, spontaneous love terrifies the student but does not run away with him . . . loses her faithful lover Rakitin, remains with her husband, for whom she has respect but no love'. The part could only be successfully acted by dividing it into segments: in one segment Natalya Petrovna is amusing, charming, enthusiastic, untroubled; in the next segment she is at the beginning of a new mood – jealousy, suspicion, uneasiness, and the like. Other constant changes of tone, feeling and mood follow, carefully separated from each other, like the movements of a symphony, by the director who (so he tells us) obeyed his instinct as an actor and tried to forget his role as director. Stanislavsky's dominant influence established a tradition of psychological realism in the production of this play which was preserved for a number of years in Russia, and remains to this day the most usual approach to it in the West.

As in the case of all works of art of the first order, more than one interpretation can be valid. It would have been particularly surprising if, in the case of Turgenev, no thought had been given to the possibility of the presence of social and political ideas in this play. A purely aesthetic approach to it as being, above all, the work of an exquisite stylist who wrote with lyrical feeling, touched with nostalgia, about the last enchantments of the life of the declining Russian gentry, as the creation of the incomparable artist so deeply admired by Flaubert and Henry James and (until he discovered what he had written about him) Alphonse Daudet – this approach rests on a just assessment of one side of Turgenev's artistic personality. At the same time, like all other Russian writers of any stature in the mid nineteenth century, he was profoundly concerned with the condition of his country, and his major novels made their impact on the Russian public as much by their social content as by their artistic quality. He became, perhaps more than he cared to be, the object of political controversy in his country, and it would have been astonishing if a play written by him in revolutionary Paris, immediately after the death of the great radical tribune Belinsky (to whose memory, both as a man and a critic, Turgenev remained devoted all of his life) had been without any political implications. Soviet critics, naturally enough, have emphasised, indeed, greatly over-emphasised, this element in this and Turgenev's other plays of the period. But whatever one's conception of *A Month in the Country*, a strong undercurrent of social criticism is intrinsic to it; to ignore this aspect of the drama is to fail in understanding. The line taken by Soviet and other Marxist commentators is to play down the traditional interpretation of the central theme, as the destructive effect on an entire household of a purely emotional crisis undergone by a handsome, rich, clever, discontented woman. Natalya Petrovna has no aim in life; she is bored by her surroundings, and by the helpless love of the intelligent, weak, equally aimless friend of the family, Rakitin. She falls in love with her small son's young tutor, a simple, natural, vigorous, somewhat naive university student, who is, in his turn, excited and confused by the strong, elegant, physically attractive, infatuated landowner's wife. To forward her plans, she makes use of a venal factotum, the astute, corrupt, cynical doctor. Her jealous pursuit of the student ruins the happiness of her innocent ward, who loves him too, loves him unhappily. In turn ruthless, uncertain of her feelings, and racked by guilt, Natalya Petrovna wreaks havoc upon all who surround her, until she has no alternative left but to return in a mood of bleak humiliation to her troubled and unloved husband. This is how the play was, for the most part, understood by actors and directors in Russia before the Revolution, and in the West until our own day. This follows Stanislavsky's 'psychological' interpretation of the play, and there is no reason to doubt that this is how the author himself saw it.

But for Soviet critics and directors during the last fifty years, the heart of the matter is not this at all. Rather, they have tended to see it in the confrontation of two social groups: on one side the tired, decadent, feckless, morally bankrupt class of the declining gentry – represented by Natalya Petrovna, Rakitin, Anna Semyonovna, Bolshintsov – the last relics of a collapsing, semi-feudal regime, whose fate is sealed, doomed as they are to destruction by the forces of history; and on the other side, Belyaev, Vera, the servant-girl Katya, even Matvei, and up to a point Islayev, who are positive, healthy, capable, industrious, made for life and work and happiness. Whatever condition these last may be in now, they are the forerunners of the 'new men' of Chernyshevsky's famous novel, *What Is To Be Done?*, (which influenced so many Russian revolutionaries), embodiments of the forces of progress – they alone will inherit the earth and will deserve to do so. The doctor, Shpigelsky, although he has sold himself to the gentry, is a resentful casualty of the class struggle: he is aware of the stupidity and viciousness of his masters, and is a sharp-eyed witness of the process of their decay, which he notes with vindictive pleasure.

This interpretation has been driven too far, nevertheless there is a great deal of truth in it. The censored passages are clear evidence of the direction of Turgenev's social analysis in the play: Shpigelsky's sarcasms about an officer of the Imperial army; his open admission of his hypocrisy towards the gentry, towards the landowners whom he deceives because they are stupid and ridiculous, but without whose patronage he cannot survive; his mocking words about 'backwoodsmen' who only stopped 'neighing not so long ago'; his bitter account of his childhood, when he was hungry and cold and barefoot; of his mother's wretched condition; his glancing reference to the fact that he was not born in wedlock; his resentment of patronage; his deep and indelible hatred of the benefactor who helped him to make his way – his citing of all these facts in order to explain his dishonesty, as well as his grovelling before the rich and powerful, to whom he knows himself to be intellectually superior and his savage remarks about the management of his household by his future wife – all this amounts to a bitter indictment of a social system which no reader, no member of a theatrical audience in Russia in the nineteenth century, could have missed. It was something which even the stupidest censors were bound to notice, particularly during the severe reaction which, in Russia, followed the European revolutions of 1848. As for the student Belyaev, he is a mild, but nevertheless clear, prototype of the members of that classless dissident intelligentsia with which Turgenev was in sympathy all his life. In the first draft, which Turgenev corrected, Belyaev was described as a student belonging to the 'department of political studies' of the university. 'Department of political studies' was removed by Turgenev, 'university' was crossed out by the censor. The periodical which Belyaev asks Rakitin to lend him is obviously somewhat radical in character, since it is one in which 'a warm-hearted man' (in this context a clear reference to Belinsky) writes his critical articles – indeed, it is not too far-fetched to suggest that the name of Belyaev is an echo of that of Turgenev's dead friend and mentor. Belinsky's name could not for many years be mentioned openly in Russia, any more than that of Herzen: but Turgenev shows his hand clearly enough when he makes Belyaev speak of his inability to concentrate on any one subject, his ignorance of French, his faulty translations from it, work which he is forced to undertake in order to keep alive, his enthusiasm for George Sand – all of which was true of Belinsky as a young man. Belyaev is gentle, friendly, easily upset; Bazarov, in *Fathers and Sons*, is rude and formidable, but they are both self-made men, members of the intelligentsia, springing from the same social milieu, socially sensitive, with a positivist outlook, uninterested in poetry or fiction – representatives of a trend with which Turgenev was preoccupied in *Rudin* and *Smoke* and *Virgin Soil*. It was, indeed, his obvious sympathy, however qualified, with the new generation, that was the main reason why the government ordered that his funeral in St Petersburg be conducted under police surveillance, for fear of a left-wing demonstration. Rakitin does not attack the social system or align himself with its critics. But his outburst to the student, in the last act of the play, when he tells him that all love, whether happy or unhappy, is a calamity for those who surrender to it completely, was evidently too bitter for the censor. He speaks about the humiliation, slavery and torment of those who love; he tells Belyaev that independence is what matters, that if the pleasures of life – love, or simply desire, on the part of a woman – ever come his way, he must not hesitate, must grasp them with both hands. He goes on to warn him that all deviation from the commonplaces of daily life is invariably punished. He is, in effect, uttering a passionate denunciation of conventional social ethics, particularly of family morality. Whether or not it was inspired by Turgenev's own ambivalent position in the household of the singer Pauline Viardot, whom he loved until the end of his life (his relationship with her husband was in some respects not unlike that of Rakitin and Islayev), or by the views of his friend of those days, the future anarchist Bakunin, this kind of thing could clearly not be allowed on the stage, and scarcely in a published text accessible to the general public. The only other type of objection which the censor raised was against what appeared to him to be coarse language or the illicit use of religious terminology – Rakitin could not be allowed to say to Natalya Petrovna that she had been 'transfigured', nor Anna Semyonovna to address herself to God in solemn, religious terminology in a trivial domestic situation.

There has been no mention, so far as I know, of these pronounced social and political features of the play either in Russian writing before the Revolution, or in Western literary history or criticism. But to the readers of *The Contemporary* and similar publications, to the 'men of the forties', the first generation of socially concerned Russian liberal writers and readers, in whose company Turgenev's youth was spent, these issues were all too familiar. *A Month in the Country* may be approached in many ways, but if either the psychological realism of the 'comedy' (it is difficult to say why Turgenev called it so) or the faith of the intelligentsia incorporated in it are ignored, the point of the play, the purpose of the writer will be missed. It is not political, nor is it overtly, or even principally, concerned with specific social issues; but it seems to me to be more radical in tone, to contain more social protest, than any play by Ostrovsky or Chekhov, for all the explicit social content of their dramatic works. One of the earliest of Turgenev's post-Revolutionary critics, in the course of discussing the evolution of the ideas of the Russian intelligentsia, said that 'the development of social thought in Russia from the forties to the eighties of the nineteenth century can be learnt from the novels of Ivan Sergeyevich Turgenev'.* This is not an opinion commonly found among Western literary historians; nevertheless, I believe it to be true.

In translating Turgenev's text I was guided by one paramount consideration: to find the most precise English equivalent of the author's simple, natural, limpid Russian; it is the purest and most classical after the greatest, and most unattainable, of his masters, Alexander Pushkin. In doing this, I made no attempt to imitate the style of mid-Victorian English writers, with whose prose Turgenev's seems to me to have little in common, or, on the other hand, to try to obliterate the distance that separates the modern reader from a more than century-old past by deliberately introducing the idioms and colloquialisms of our own day. Turgenev's dialogue seems to me to convey the rhythm and style of Russian speech as it was still spoken in much of the twentieth century, and indeed, can still be heard here and there today. I have done my best to make the translation as transparent and self-effacing as possible, while at the same time avoiding any attempt to make the characters talk in too obviously English a fashion. How far I have succeeded in this is not for me to judge.

* Mikhail Portugalov, *Turgeniana*, p. 45, Gosizdat, Orel, USSR, 1922.

I have received help from many sources, and would like to acknowledge this as fully as I can. To begin with, I owe a debt to earlier translators. There were a number of passages in my first draft with which I was dissatisfied. In such cases, I tended to consult the versions of Constance Garnett (whose services to Russian literature, as translator, remain unique) and Ariadnae Nicolaeff, and, where they seemed to me to have solved a particular problem better than I had been able to do, I did not hesitate to use perhaps as many as half-a-dozen of their most felicitous sentences or single words in my text. Miss Nicolaeff's prose was in general too racy for me, but at times she succeeded splendidly. As for Mrs Garnett, I should like to mention two particularly good examples of truly successful renderings: in the course of Rakitin's last bitter speech to Belyaev about the torments and humiliations of hopeless infatuation, he tells him that he does not know what it is 'to be the property of a skirt' – that is the literal translation, but it will surely not do as it stands. After despairing of finding an exact English equivalent, I began to depart from it altogether in favour of such expressions as 'to be a woman's slave' or 'a mere chattel', and the like. Mrs Garnett provides 'to be tied to a petticoat', which appears to me exactly right. And again, when Islayev asks his butler Matvei whether he has seen Rakitin anywhere, Matvei (who is a serf) replies 'They are in the library' – the plural 'they' is the only way in which a serf, perhaps any servant in Russia in the 1850s, could refer to a member of the gentry, but this will not do in English. After casting about for social equivalents, I was prepared to settle for 'The gentleman is in the library', but Mrs Garnett's 'his honour' seems to me just right, socially and historically. I only quote these instances to indicate the kind of help that I received from my gifted predecessors.

The version I used was the simple but excellent edition of the Russian text by T. A. Greenan, of the University of Liverpool. (The Library of Russian Classics, Bradda Books Ltd, 1971.) Mr Greenan's introduction is a model of its kind, and his notes and vocabulary seem to me most useful, not merely for university students, but for anyone who may wish to read and understand the play. He is, fortunately, one of the commentators who have not been affected by Turgenev's own disparagement of his talents as a playwright, or have considered A Month in the Country as being of interest mainly as an anticipation of Chekhov's plays, but on the contrary, as being the equal of Turgenev's most finished master-pieces – an opinion which I fully share.

I must also acknowledge a very considerable debt to Mr Peter Gill, who produced the play for the National Theatre in London, and who supplied me with the changes which he and the artists who acted in it had made for the stage version: some of these seemed to me better than my original version, and I incorporated them gratefully in my text. My friends, the Marchioness of Anglesey, Lord and Lady Donaldson, Mr Ian McGilchrist and Mrs Patricia Utechin, read one or other of the drafts and I wish to offer my thanks to them, and most especially to my wife, who read the text more than once, for their suggestions, which I found most valuable. My thanks are also due to Mrs Harriet Smith and Dr Anthony Smith for permitting their painting by Mstislav Doboujinsky – one of his designs for display at the Moscow Art Theatre production of 1909 – to be reproduced on the jacket of this volume. Finally, I acknowledge my debt to Sir Peter Hall for offering me this commis-sion: it gave me many anxious and absorbing hours for which I wish to thank him.

ISAIAH BERLIN
Oxford, April, 1981

A MONTH IN THE COUNTRY

A comedy in five acts

ARKADI SERGEYEVICH ISLAYEV, a rich landowner, 36 years old
NATALYA PETROVNA, his wife, 29
KOLYA, their son, 10
VERA ALEKSANDROVNA (Verochka), Natalya Petrovna's ward, 17
ANNA SEMYONOVNA ISLAYEVA, Islayev's mother, 58
LIZAVETA BOGDANOVNA, a companion, 37
ADAM IVANOVICH SCHAAF, a German tutor, 45
MIKHAILO ALEKSANDROVICH RAKITIN, a family friend, 30
ALEKSEI NIKOLAYEVICH BELYAEV, a student, Kolya's tutor, 21
AFANASI IVANOVICH BOLSHINTSOV, a neighbour, 48
IGNATI ILYICH SHPIGELSKY, a doctor, 40
MATVEI, a servant, 40
KATYA, a servant, 20

The action takes place on Islayev's estate at the beginning of the 1840s. Intervals of a day or so pass between Acts One and Two, between Two and Three, and between Four and Five.

ACT ONE

The sitting-room. On the right, a card-table, and door to the study; centre, a door into the hall; left, two windows and a round table. In the corner, sofas. Anna Semyonovna, Lizaveta Bogdanovna and Schaaf are at the card-table; they are playing préférence.[1] *Natalya Petrovna and Rakitin are sitting near the round table. Natalya Petrovna is doing needlework, Rakitin has a book in his hands. The clock on the wall says three o'clock.*

SCHAAF: Harrds.

ANNA SEMYONOVNA: What, again? If you go on like this, dear friend, that will be the end of us.

SCHAAF *impassively:* Eighdd ov harrrds.

ANNA SEMYONOVNA *to Lizaveta Bogdanovna:* Oh lord! It's impossible to play with him. *Lizaveta Bogdanovna smiles.*

NATALYA PETROVNA *to Rakitin:* Why have you stopped? Go on reading.

RAKITIN *lifting the book slowly: Monte-Cristo se redressa haletant.*[2] Natalya Petrovna, do you find this interesting?

NATALYA PETROVNA: Not at all.

RAKITIN: Then why are you reading it?

NATALYA PETROVNA: I'll tell you why. The other day a lady said to me 'You haven't read *Monte-Cristo*? Oh, you must read it, it is delightful.' I said nothing to her at the time, but now I can tell her that I *have* read it, and did not find it in the least delightful.

RAKITIN: Oh well, if you've managed to convince yourself already . . .

NATALYA PETROVNA: Goodness, how lazy you are!

RAKITIN: Oh, I am so sorry, I am perfectly ready. *Finding his place in the book. Se redressa haletant et . . .*

NATALYA PETROVNA *interrupting him:* Have you seen Arkadi today?

RAKITIN: I met him at the weir: they're repairing it; he was trying to explain something to the workmen, and to make it clearer he waded into the sand up to his knees –

---

1 A three-handed game resembling whist in which the trump is determined by bidding.

2 Monte-Cristo leapt up panting.

NATALYA PETROVNA: He throws himself into *everything* – he takes up everything with too much passion – he tries too hard – that's a fault, don't you think?

RAKITIN: Yes, I agree.

NATALYA PETROVNA: Oh, how boring . . . You always agree with me. Do go on reading.

RAKITIN: I see, so you want me to argue with you . . . very well.

NATALYA PETROVNA: I *want*, I *want* . . . I want *you* to want: read, I tell you.

RAKITIN: Yes, ma'am. *Begins the book again.*

SCHAAF: Harrds.

ANNA SEMYONOVNA: What? Again? This is intolerable. *To Natalya Petrovna.* Natasha . . . Natasha . . .

NATALYA PETROVNA: What is it?

ANNA SEMYONOVNA: Can you believe it, Schaaf has completely trounced us – seven of hearts, eight of hearts, one after the other.

SCHAAF: Dis dime alzo zeven.

ANNA SEMYONOVNA: Do you hear? This is appalling.

NATALYA PETROVNA: Yes . . . appalling.

ANNA SEMYONOVNA: That's whist for you. *To Natalya Petrovna.* And where's Kolya?

NATALYA PETROVNA: He's gone for a walk with the new tutor.

ANNA SEMYONOVNA: I see. Lizaveta Bogdanovna, may I invite you . . . ?

RAKITIN *to Natalya Petrovna:* What tutor?

NATALYA PETROVNA: Oh yes, of course, I forgot to tell you. We engaged a new tutor without consulting you.

RAKITIN: To replace Dufour?

NATALYA PETROVNA: No . . . a Russian tutor. The Princess is sending us a Frenchman from Moscow.

RAKITIN: What sort of man is this Russian tutor? Old?

NATALYA PETROVNA: No, young . . . incidentally, we've only taken him for the summer.

RAKITIN: Ah, it's a vacation job?

NATALYA PETROVNA: Yes, I think that's what they call it. And do you know something, Rakitin? I know you love observing people, dissecting them, going deeply into them.

RAKITIN: No, really, why? What makes you think . . . ?

NATALYA PETROVNA: Oh yes, yes. Take a look at him: I like him.

Thin, good figure, cheerful-looking, bold expression. You'll see. It's true, he's rather awkward . . . and you can't bear that . . .

RAKITIN: Natalya Petrovna, you really are persecuting me today.

NATALYA PETROVNA: No, but seriously, do pay him some attention. I think he has the makings of a very nice man. Although God knows one never can tell.

RAKITIN: You do arouse my curiosity.

NATALYA PETROVNA: Really? *Thoughtfully.* Do read.

RAKITIN: *Se redressa haletant et* . . .

NATALYA PETROVNA *looking round suddenly:* Where is Vera? I haven't seen her since this morning. *Smiling to Rakitin.* Oh, do throw away that book, I can see that we aren't going to get any reading done today; better tell me about something.

RAKITIN: Very well; what can I tell you about? I expect you know that I spent a few days at the Krinitsyns . . . would you believe it, the young couple are bored already.

NATALYA PETROVNA: How do you know?

RAKITIN: Do you think that one can conceal boredom – anything else, yes, but not boredom.

NATALYA PETROVNA: *Anything* else?

RAKITIN *after a silence:* I think so.

NATALYA PETROVNA *lowering her eyes:* Well, what were you doing at the Krinitsyns?

RAKITIN: Nothing. To be bored by friends is a terrible thing: you don't feel embarrassed, there's no constraint, you love them, you have nothing to be cross about, and yet boredom gnaws at you; and your heart aches idiotically, as if from hunger.

NATALYA PETROVNA: You are often bored with your friends, I see.

RAKITIN: As if you didn't know what it is to be in the presence of someone you love and yet who bores you stiff.

NATALYA PETROVNA: 'Love', that's a powerful word. You're being a bit too clever for me.

RAKITIN: Too clever? Why too clever?

NATALYA PETROVNA: Yes, that is one of your faults. D'you know, Rakitin, you are, of course, very clever . . . but *(a pause)*, at times, when we are talking together, it's as though we were lace-making . . . Have you ever seen lace-makers at work? They sit in airless rooms, without moving from their places. Lace is a wonderful thing, but a drink of fresh water on a hot day is better still.

RAKITIN: Natalya Petrovna, today you are . . .

NATALYA PETROVNA: What?

RAKITIN: You are angry with me about something.

NATALYA PETROVNA: Oh you clever people, how little insight you have, for all your subtlety! No, I am not angry with you.

ANNA SEMYONOVNA: Ah! At last he's done it! He's revoked. *To Natalya Petrovna.* Natasha, our villain has revoked.

SCHAAF *sourly:* It's ze follt of Lissafet Poktanovna.

LIZAVETA BOGDANOVNA *irritably:* I am sorry, but I could not know that Anna Semyonovna had no hearts.

SCHAAF: Neffer again Lissafet Poktanovna to be mein bardner vill I infide.

ANNA SEMYONOVNA *to Schaaf:* But what fault is it of hers?

SCHAAF *repeats in precisely the same tone of voice:* Neffer again Lissafet Poktanovna to be mein bardner vill I infide.

LIZAVETA BOGDANOVNA: As if I cared! This really is too much!

RAKITIN: The more I look at you, Natalya Petrovna, the less I recognise your face today.

NATALYA PETROVNA *with some curiosity:* Oh, really?

RAKITIN: I assure you. I find a certain change in you.

NATALYA PETROVNA: Oh? In that case, do me a favour . . . after all, you know me – would you venture a guess about what exactly this change might be. What it is that has taken place in me?

RAKITIN: If you'll wait a moment . . .

Kolya runs in noisily from the hall, straight to Anna Semyonovna.

KOLYA: Grandmama, Grandmama, look at what I've got. *Shows her a bow and arrow.* Do look.

ANNA SEMYONOVNA: Show me, darling . . . Oh, what a lovely bow! Who made it for you?

KOLYA: There he is – him. *Points to Belyaev, who remains standing by the door to the hall.*

ANNA SEMYONOVNA: And how beautifully he has made it.

KOLYA: Oh yes, I've been shooting with it already, at a tree, Grandmama. I hit it twice. *Jumps up and down.*

NATALYA PETROVNA: Show me, Kolya.

Kolya runs up to her, and while Natalya Petrovna is examining the bow, speaks.

KOLYA: Oh, Mama, you should see how Aleksei Nikolaich climbs trees! He wants to teach me how to, and he's going to teach me to swim too. He'll teach me everything, everything! *Leaps about.*

NATALYA PETROVNA *to Belyaev:* I am most grateful to you for being so attentive to Kolya.

KOLYA *interrupting her ardently:* I like him very much, Mama, very, very much.

NATALYA PETROVNA *stroking Kolya's head:* I've made him a little bit too soft — you must make him a more vigorous, a more active boy for me. *Belyaev bows.*

KOLYA: Aleksei Nikolaich, let's go to the stables and take some bread to Favourite — let's go.

ANNA SEMYONOVNA *to Kolya:* First come here and give me a kiss.

KOLYA *running away:* Later, Grandmama, later. *Runs into the hall. Belyaev follows him.*

ANNA SEMYONOVNA *looking after Kolya:* What a sweet child! *To Schaaf and Lizaveta Bogdanovna.* Isn't he?

LIZAVETA BOGDANOVNA: Why, yes, indeed, ma'am.

SCHAAF *after a silence:* I passing.

NATALYA PETROVNA *to Rakitin, with a certain animation:* Well, what did you think of him?

RAKITIN: Of whom?

NATALYA PETROVNA *after a silence:* This — this Russian tutor.

RAKITIN: Oh, I beg your pardon, I quite forgot ... I am so preoccupied with the question you set me. *Natalya Petrovna looks at him with a scarcely visible mocking smile.* Well, yes, his face, yes, actually, yes, he has got a good face. I like him. Only he does seem extremely shy.

NATALYA PETROVNA: Yes.

RAKITIN *looking at her:* But still, I am not quite clear about him, I'm not sure.

NATALYA PETROVNA: Shall we do something about him, Rakitin? Shall we finish his education? What an excellent opportunity for sensible, staid people like you and me: we are very sensible, don't you think?

RAKITIN: This young man interests you. If he knew it — he would be very flattered.

NATALYA PETROVNA: Oh no, believe me, not at all: one can't judge him by what someone like us would feel in his place; he's very unlike us, Rakitin. That's the trouble, my friend: we examine ourselves in the minutest detail, and then imagine that we know what other people are like.

RAKITIN: 'The souls of others are a dark forest'. What are all these mysterious hints – why these pinpricks all the time?

NATALYA PETROVNA: Whom can one tease if it isn't one's friends? And you *are* my friend . . . you know you are. *Presses his hand. Rakitin smiles and his face lights up.* My old friend.

RAKITIN: It's only that I'm afraid . . . that you may have had too much of this old friend.

NATALYA PETROVNA *laughing:* It's only good things one can have too much of.

RAKITIN: That may be, but it doesn't help them much.

NATALYA PETROVNA: Oh, come . . . *(lowering her voice)* as though you didn't know *ce que vous êtes pour moi.*[1]

RAKITIN: Natalya Petrovna, you are playing with me, playing cat and mouse; but the mouse is not complaining.

NATALYA PETROVNA: Oh, the poor little mouse.

ANNA SEMYONOVNA: Twenty from you, Adam Ivanych . . . Ah ha!

SCHAAF: Neffer again Lissafet Poktanovna to be mein bardner I vill infide.

MATVEI *entering from the hall, announces:* Ignati Ilyich has arrived, ma'am.

SHPIGELSKY *following him:* Doctors aren't announced. *Matvei goes out.* My humble duty to the entire family. *Goes up to Anna Semyonovna and kisses her hand.* How are you, dear lady? Winning, I expect?

ANNA SEMYONOVNA: Winning indeed! I've only just avoided total ruin . . . Thank God for *that* – it's all this villain's doing. *Points to Schaaf.*

SHPIGELSKY *to Schaaf:* Adam Ivanych, you've been behaving like this to ladies? Not very nice – I can't believe it of you –

SCHAAF *muttering through his teeth:* Do laties, do laties . . .

SHPIGELSKY *goes up to the round table on the left:* How do you do, Natalya Petrovna, how do you do, Mikhailo Aleksandrych.

NATALYA PETROVNA: How do you do, Doctor, are you well?

SHPIGELSKY: I'm glad you asked me that, for it means that you are well. How am I? A good doctor is never ill; although, of course, he may suddenly go and die – ha, ha.

1 What you are to me.

NATALYA PETROVNA: Do sit down. Yes, I *am* well . . . But I'm in a bad mood . . . that is a kind of ill health, too.

SHPIGELSKY *settling himself near Natalya Petrovna:* Allow me, may I take your pulse? *Feels the pulse.* Oh dear, it's nerves, nerves . . . You don't walk much, Natalya Petrovna . . . and you don't laugh much . . . that's what it is . . . Mikhailo Aleksandrych, why are you staring? Oh well, I think white drops are indicated; I'd better give you a prescription.

NATALYA PETROVNA: I've nothing against laughter. *With animation.* Now, Doctor, you . . . you have a wicked tongue, and I love and respect you for that . . . I do indeed . . . Do tell me something amusing. Mikhailo Aleksandrych philosophises all day long.

SHPIGELSKY *glancing at Rakitin out of the corner of his eye:* Ah, I see it's not only nerves, there's also a tiny overflow of bile.

NATALYA PETROVNA: You too! Do as much observing as you like, but not aloud, I beg of you! We all know that you are terribly perceptive . . . you are both very, very perceptive.

SHPIGELSKY: Your humble servant.

NATALYA PETROVNA: Tell us something amusing.

SHPIGELSKY: At your command: but I had no notion . . . no conception . . . this is so sudden – out of the blue – hey presto, tell us a story! May I take some snuff, dear lady? *Takes it.*

NATALYA PETROVNA: What elaborate preparations!

SHPIGELSKY: But, dearest lady, Natalya Petrovna, you must realise that there is humour and humour: people's tastes differ; your neighbour, for instance, Mr Khlopushkin: all you have to do is show him a finger, like that – and he bursts out laughing, shrieks, chokes, cries, tears roll down his cheeks: whereas you . . . However, with your kind permission – do you know Verenitsyn – Platon Vassilyevich?

NATALYA PETROVNA: I think I do, or at least, have heard of him.

SHPIGELSKY: He had a sister, quite mad. I think they are either both mad or both perfectly sane; because there is absolutely no difference between them: however, that is not my point. Fate, 'tis always fate, it governs everything. Verenitsyn has a daughter, pale green, if you know what I mean, pale little eyes, pink little nose, yellow little teeth, in short a charming young lady: plays the piano and *lisps* – it's all exactly as it should be. She owns two hundred souls, plus her aunt's hundred and fifty. The aunt is still alive and will live for years – the mad always do – every cloud has that kind of silver lining. She's going to leave everything to her niece. The other day I poured some cold water over the aunt's head with my own hands – quite pointless, since there isn't the slightest possibility of a cure. So you can see that Verenitsyn's girl is really quite a desirable match. Her father began to take her about and suitors began to appear, among them one Perekuzov, a sickly youth, rather timid but most virtuous. Well, the father liked this man Perekuzov, and the daughter did too . . . So, why wait? To the altar, with God's blessing. Everything was going beautifully. Mr Verenitsyn, Platon Vassilich, began poking Mr Perekuzov in the stomach, patted his shoulder and that sort of thing, when suddenly out of the blue who should appear but an officer, on his way somewhere else, one Ardalion Protobekasov. The Verenitsyn girl met him at the country ball: he dances three polkas with her, probably rolls his eyes at her with a melting look, says 'Oh, how unhappy I am' – the girl immediately goes off her head. Tears, sighs, groans . . . we don't look at Perekuzov any more, don't talk to him, the mere mention of the wedding causes a fit. Goodness me, what an appalling situation! Well, thinks Verenitsyn, if it's to be Protobekasov, so be it, especially since he too is a man of means. Protobekasov is invited – may we have the honour – the officer is only too willing; arrives; courts the lady; falls in love, finally offers her his hand and his heart. What do you suppose happens now? Our young lady, overjoyed, accepts at once? Far from it. Lord preserve us, more tears, sighs, fainting fits. The father doesn't know where to turn. What is it? What does she want, for God's sake? Well, what do you think she answers him? That she doesn't know which of them she loves, this one or that one: 'What?' 'I swear to God, I don't know. I'd better not marry anybody, but I *am* in love, I am, I am.' Verenitsyn, of course, is completely stunned. The suitors don't know what to expect, she won't budge: she says the same thing over and over again. That's the kind of thing that's going on in our corner of the world. Don't you think it's fascinating?

NATALYA PETROVNA: I don't find it odd . . . as if one can't love two people at once . . .

RAKITIN: Ah, you think . . .

NATALYA PETROVNA *slowly:* I think – no, I don't know . . . Perhaps it only shows that one doesn't love either one.

SHPIGELSKY *taking snuff and glancing now at Natalya Petrovna, now at Rakitin:* I see, I see . . .

NATALYA PETROVNA *with animation, to Shpigelsky:* It's a very good story, but you haven't made me laugh.

SHPIGELSKY: But, dear lady, who could possibly make you laugh at the moment? That's not what you need now.

NATALYA PETROVNA: What do I need?

SHPIGELSKY *with mock humility:* The Lord only knows.

NATALYA PETROVNA: What a bore you are, no better than Rakitin.

SHPIGELSKY: Too much honour, dear lady. *Natalya Petrovna makes a gesture of impatience.*

ANNA SEMYONOVNA *rising from her seat:* Oh, at long last . . . *Sighs.* I've cramp in my legs, pins and needles. *Lizaveta Bogdanovna and Schaaf also rise.* Oh-h-h.

NATALYA PETROVNA *getting up and walking towards them:* Well, if you will sit there all this time . . . *Shpigelsky and Rakitin get up.*

ANNA SEMYONOVNA *to Schaaf:* You owe me seventy kopeks, my good man *(Schaaf bows drily),* you can't do us down all the time, you know. *To Natalya Petrovna.* You look a little pale today, Natasha, are you well? Shpigelsky, is she well?

SHPIGELSKY *who is whispering about something with Rakitin:* Oh, oh yes, absolutely.

ANNA SEMYONOVNA: Oh good . . . I'll go and rest a little before dinner . . . I'm terribly tired. Liza, come, . . . oh, my legs, my legs. *Goes with Lizaveta Bogdanovna to the hall; Natalya Petrovna accompanies her to the door; Shpigelsky, Rakitin and Schaaf remain in front of the stage.*

SHPIGELSKY *to Schaaf, offering his snuffbox:* Well, Adam Ivanych, *wie befinden Sie sich?*[1]

SCHAAF *taking snuff with an air of importance:* Vell. And you are how?

SHPIGELSKY: Thank you kindly, not too bad. *To Rakitin, in a low voice.* Do you really not know what is the matter with Natalya Petrovna today?

RAKITIN: No, I really have no idea.

SHPIGELSKY: Oh well, if *you* don't know. *Turns, and goes to meet Natalya Petrovna, who is returning from the door.* I have a small matter to discuss with you, Natalya Petrovna.

1 And how are you?

NATALYA PETROVNA *moving to the window:* Really? What is it?

SHPIGELSKY: I must talk to you in private.

NATALYA PETROVNA: Oh . . . indeed? You terrify me.

In the meanwhile, Rakitin puts his arm through Schaaf's and walks up and down with him and whispers something to him in German: Schaaf laughs.

SCHAFF *in a low voice: Ja, ja, jawohl, jawohl, sehr gut.*[1]

SHPIGELSKY *lowering his voice:* Actually, you are not the only one involved in this matter . . .

NATALYA PETROVNA *looking at the garden:* What are you trying to say?

SHPIGELSKY: Oh well, the thing is this: someone I know quite well asked me to find out . . . er . . . that is . . . to ask you about . . . about your intentions concerning your ward, Vera Aleksandrovna.

NATALYA PETROVNA: My intentions?

SHPIGELSKY: I mean . . . may I be quite frank . . . my acquaintance . . .

NATALYA PETROVNA: Does he want to marry her?

SHPIGELSKY: Precisely.

NATALYA PETROVNA: Are you joking?

SHPIGELSKY: No, ma'am, not at all.

NATALYA PETROVNA *laughing:* For goodness sake! She's still a child – what a strange errand.

SHPIGELSKY: But why strange, Natalya Petrovna . . .? My acquaintance –

NATALYA PETROVNA: What a cunning dealer you are, Shpigelsky – who is this friend of yours?

SHPIGELSKY *smiling:* Oh, please, I beg you . . . but can you not tell me anything definite?

NATALYA PETROVNA: Come, come, Doctor, Vera is still a child, you know that perfectly well, *Monsieur le diplomate. Turning.* And here she is herself, how appropriate. *Vera and Kolya run in from the hall.*

KOLYA *running up to Rakitin:* Rakitin, tell them to give us some glue, some glue.

NATALYA PETROVNA *to Vera:* Where have you been? *Strokes her cheek.* How flushed you are.

1 Yes, yes, of course, of course, very good.

VERA: In the garden. *Shpigelsky bows to her.* How do you do, Ignati Ilyich.

RAKITIN *to Kolya:* What do you want glue for?

KOLYA: I must have it, I must — Aleksei Nikolaich is making us a kite . . . tell them . . .

RAKITIN *makes as if to press the bell:* Wait, in a minute . . .

SCHAAF: *Erlauben Sie*[1], Mashter Koliya to-tay hass nod hiss lesson donn. *Takes Kolya by the hand. Kommen Sie.*[2]

KOLYA *gloomily: Morgen*[3], Herr Schaaf, *morgen.*

SCHAAF *sharply: Morgen, morgen, nur nich heute*
             Sagen alle faule Leute[4]
. . . *Kommen Sie.*

Kolya shows signs of resistance.

NATALYA PETROVNA *to Vera:* Who did you go for such a long walk with? I haven't seen you since this morning.

VERA: With Aleksei Nikolaich . . . and Kolya . . .

NATALYA PETROVNA: Oh! *Turning.* Kolya, what does this mean?

KOLYA *lowering his voice:* Mr Schaaf . . . Mama . . .

RAKITIN *to Natalya Petrovna:* They're making a kite over there, and he's been told that he ought to be doing his lessons.

SCHAAF *with some show of dignity: Gnädige Frau*[5] . . .

NATALYA PETROVNA *sternly, to Kolya:* Do as you are told: you've run about quite enough today — off you go with Mr Schaaf.

SCHAAF: *Es ist unerhört.*[6]

KOLYA *on his way out, in a whisper to Rakitin:* You will tell them about the glue . . . ? *Rakitin nods.*

SCHAAF *pulling at Kolya: Kommen Sie, Mein Herr*[7]. *Goes out in to hall, Rakitin follows them.*

NATALYA PETROVNA *to Vera:* Sit down . . . you must be tired.

VERA *sits down:* Not at all, ma'am.

NATALYA PETROVNA *smiling at Shpigelsky:* Shpigelsky, do look at her — she *is* tired, isn't she?

SHPIGELSKY: Yes, but it does Vera Aleksandrovna good.

1 Permit me. 2 Come. 3 Tomorrow.
4 Morrow, t'morrow, not today, That is what all idlers say.
5 Madam. 6 It's unheard of. 7 Come along, sir.

NATALYA PETROVNA: No, I don't mean . . . *To Vera.* Well, what have you been doing in the garden?

VERA: Playing, ma'am, and running about. First we watched the weir being dug, then Aleksei Nikolaich climbed up a tree after a squirrel – he went up very high and began to shake the top – we were actually rather frightened – in the end the squirrel did fall, and Trésor very nearly caught it, but it got away.

NATALYA PETROVNA *with a smile to Shpigelsky:* And then?

VERA: And then Aleksei Nikolaich made a bow for Kolya . . . in no time at all . . . and then he crept up to our cow in the meadow and suddenly leapt on its back – the cow was frightened and began running and kicking . . . but he was laughing. *Laughs herself.* Then Aleksei Nikolaich wanted to make us a kite, and then we came here.

NATALYA PETROVNA *pats her on the cheek:* Child, child, you are nothing but a child, aren't you – what do *you* think, Shpigelsky?

SHPIGELSKY *slowly, and looking at Natalya Petrovna:* I agree with you.

NATALYA PETROVNA: Well, then . . .

SHPIGELSKY: But that's no obstacle . . . on the contrary . . .

NATALYA PETROVNA: You think? *To Vera.* Did you have a wonderful time?

VERA: Yes, ma'am. It's such fun being with Aleksei Nikolaich.

NATALYA PETROVNA: Ah, I see. *After a silence.* Verochka, how old are you? *Vera looks at her with some surprise.* Child, child . . .

Rakitin enters from the hall.

SHPIGELSKY *busily:* Oh dear, I forgot, your coachman is unwell and I haven't seen him yet . . .

NATALYA PETROVNA: What's wrong with him?

SHPIGELSKY: It's a fever, nothing at all dangerous.

NATALYA PETROVNA *as he is leaving:* Will you stay to dinner with us, Doctor?

SHPIGELSKY: If I may. *Goes into the hall.*

NATALYA PETROVNA: *Mon enfant, vous feriez bien de mettre une autre robe pour le dîner.*[1] *Vera gets up.* Come here. *Kisses her on the forehead.* Child, child. *Vera kisses her hand and goes to the study.*

1 My child, you'd better put on another dress for dinner.

RAKITIN *quietly to Vera, with a wink:* I *have* sent Aleksei Nikolaich what he asked for.

VERA *softly:* Thank you ever so much, Mikhailo Aleksandrych. *She goes out.*

RAKITIN *going up to Natalya Petrovna – she gives him her hand. He instantly presses it:* At last we're alone. Natalya Petrovna, tell me, what is it?

NATALYA PETROVNA: Nothing, Michel, nothing. And if there was anything it's over now. Sit down. *Rakitin sits beside her.* It could happen to anyone – little clouds float across the sky. Why are you looking at me like that?

RAKITIN: I am looking at you . . . I am happy . . .

NATALYA PETROVNA *smiling in answer:* Open the window, Michel. How lovely it is in the garden. *Rakitin rises and opens the window.* Welcome, wind! *Laughs.* As if it was lying in wait, ready to burst in. *Looks round.* Oh . . . it has taken over the entire room . . . now you can't drive it out . . .

RAKITIN: Now you are quiet and gentle yourself, like an evening after a storm.

NATALYA PETROVNA *pensively repeating the last words:* After a storm . . . Why, has there been a storm?

RAKITIN *nodding his head:* It was gathering.

NATALYA PETROVNA: Oh really? *Looking at him, after a short silence.* Do you know, Michel, I cannot imagine anyone kinder than you – truly. *Rakitin makes as if to stop her.* No, no, do let me say it: you are understanding, you are tender and constant. You don't change. I owe you a very great deal.

RAKITIN: Natalya Petrovna, why are you saying all this to me at this moment?

NATALYA PETROVNA: I don't know. I feel cheerful, I feel at peace, don't stop me, let me go on talking.

RAKITIN *pressing her hand:* You are an angel.

NATALYA PETROVNA *laughing:* You wouldn't have said so this morning – but listen, Michel, you know me, you must forgive me. Our relationship is so pure, so sincere – and yet, not entirely natural: you and I, we have a right not only to our Arcadia, but to look the world straight in the face – yes; but *(thoughtfully)* that's why I sometimes feel wretched, wretched and uncomfortable, and I feel angry, and, like a child, I'm liable to vent my feelings on others, and particularly on you – you don't mind this very special honour?

RAKITIN: On the contrary.

NATALYA PETROVNA: Yes, sometimes one enjoys tormenting someone one loves – loves – after all, like Pushkin's Tatiana, I too can say 'Why should I seek by cunning to deceive?'

RAKITIN: Natalya Petrovna, you . . .

NATALYA PETROVNA *interrupts:* Yes . . . I love you; but can I tell you something, Rakitin? It sometimes seems strange to me that I love you . . . This feeling is so bright, so peaceful, it doesn't worry me, it warms me, but . . . *With animation.* You've never made me cry . . . and perhaps you should have . . . *Interrupting herself.* What does it mean?

RAKITIN *a little sadly:* That sort of question needs no answer.

NATALYA PETROVNA: We've known each other for a long time, you and I.

RAKITIN: Four years. Yes, we are old friends.

NATALYA PETROVNA: Friends . . . no, you are more than a friend . . .

RAKITIN: Natalya Petrovna, don't, don't touch on this – I am afraid for my happiness – it might slip through your fingers and be gone.

NATALYA PETROVNA: No . . . no . . . no. It is all because you are too kind . . . you give way to me too much – you have spoilt me . . . you are too kind, do you hear?

RAKITIN *smiles:* Very well.

NATALYA PETROVNA *gazing at him:* I don't know about you . . . I want no other happiness. Many people might envy me. *Holds out both hands to him.* Isn't that so?

RAKITIN: I am in your power – do what you like with me . . . *Islayev's voice is heard in the hall:* You *have* sent for him, haven't you?

NATALYA PETROVNA *quickly rising:* It's him: I can't face him now . . . Goodbye. *Exits to the study.*

RAKITIN *following her with his eyes:* What is this? The beginning of the end, or simply the end? *After a short silence.* Or the beginning?

Enter Islayev looking worried; he takes off his hat.

ISLAYEV: How do you do, Michel!

[34]

RAKITIN: We've met already today.

ISLAYEV: Oh, I'm so sorry . . . I've had too much to do today. *Walks up and down.* It's a funny thing – the Russian peasant is very intelligent – quick on the uptake – I have great respect for him – but sometimes you talk and talk to him, you explain and explain . . . it all seems clear enough . . . and yet it's no use . . . the Russian peasant does not have this . . . this . . .

RAKITIN: Are you still busy with the weir?

ISLAYEV: This . . . how shall I put it . . . this love of – this love of work, it simply isn't there – that's what's missing – he just won't let you tell him properly what you think: 'Oh yes, master, yes, I see, sir'; what does he see? He hasn't understood a word. Now, a German – that's a different story. Russians have no patience. All the same, I do respect the Russian peasant . . . Where's Natasha? Do you know where she is?

RAKITIN: She was here a moment ago.

ISLAYEV: What time is it? Time for dinner. I've been on my feet all day – a terrible lot to do – and I haven't yet been to the building site – God, how time flies – it's terrible – one can't get it all done in the time. *Rakitin smiles.* I see you're laughing at me, but my dear man, what can I do? One is made as one is made – I'm a thoroughly positive kind of fellow, born to be in charge of things – that, and nothing else. Time was – I dreamt of other things, but it just didn't work. I burnt my fingers, burnt them badly – why isn't Belyaev here?

RAKITIN: Who is Belyaev?

ISLAYEV: He's our new tutor, the Russian tutor. He seems to be an unsociable sort of fellow, but he'll get used to us – he's no fool. I asked him to go and look at the building site today. *Enter Belyaev.* . . . Ah, there he is! Well? Anybody there? Nothing's being done, I suppose?

BELYAEV: Oh no; they're working.

ISLAYEV: Have they finished the second frame?

BELYAEV: They've started on the third.

ISLAYEV: The beams, have you told them?

BELYAEV: I have.

ISLAYEV: Well, what did they say?

BELYAEV: They say that's what they always do, they've always done it like that.

ISLAYEV: Mmm . . . Is the carpenter – Yermil – is he there?

BELYAEV: He is.

ISLAYEV: Oh well, much obliged to you. *Enter Natalya Petrovna.* Ah, Natasha, and how are you?

RAKITIN: Why are you greeting everybody twenty times today?

ISLAYEV: I've told you, I'm terribly overworked; oh, by the way, have I shown you my new winnowing machine? Come and see it, do: it's well worth seeing – can you imagine, it's like a hurricane, a real hurricane; we have time before dinner – won't you come?

RAKITIN: If you like.

ISLAYEV: And you, Natasha, won't you come with us?

NATALYA PETROVNA: I know nothing about your machines – no, you go, but don't be late, will you?

ISLAYEV *leaving with Rakitin:* We won't — we'll be back in no time. *Belyaev is about to go with them.*

NATALYA PETROVNA *to Belyaev:* Where are you off to, Aleksei Nikolaich?

BELYAEV: Madam . . . I am . . .

NATALYA PETROVNA: Well, of course, if you want a walk . . .

BELYAEV: No, madam, I was out all morning.

NATALYA PETROVNA: Oh, well, in that case won't you sit down . . . sit here. *Points to a chair.* We haven't had a proper talk, Aleksei Nikolaich, we haven't got to know each other. *Belyaev bows, and sits down.* And I'd like us to get to know each other.

BELYAEV: I – madam is very flattering . . .

NATALYA PETROVNA *smiling:* You're frightened of me now, I can see that, but have patience – when you get to know me, you won't be frightened. Tell me . . . tell me, how old are you?

BELYAEV: Twenty-one, madam.

NATALYA PETROVNA: Are your parents living?

BELYAEV: My mother is dead, my father is alive.

NATALYA PETROVNA: Did your mother die a long time ago?

BELYAEV: Yes, madam.

NATALYA PETROVNA: But you remember her?

BELYAEV: Yes, of course I remember her, madam.

NATALYA PETROVNA: And your father, he lives in Moscow?

BELYAEV: No, madam, he lives in the country.

NATALYA PETROVNA: You have brothers, sisters?

BELYAEV: One sister.

NATALYA PETROVNA: Are you very fond of her?

BELYAEV: Yes, madam, she is much younger than I am.

NATALYA PETROVNA: What is her name?

BELYAEV: Natalya.

NATALYA PETROVNA *with animation:* Natalya! How curious, my name is Natalya too. *Stops.* And you love her very much?

BELYAEV: Yes, madam.

NATALYA PETROVNA: Tell me, how did you find my Kolya?

BELYAEV: He's a very nice boy.

NATALYA PETROVNA: Isn't he! And so affectionate, he's devoted to you already.

BELYAEV: I'll do what I can . . . I am happy to . . .

NATALYA PETROVNA: You see, Aleksei Nikolaich, I am naturally anxious to make a practical man of him. I don't know if I'll succeed, but in any case, I should like him to have happy memories of his childhood. Let him grow up free – that is the main thing. I was brought up very differently, Aleksei Nikolaich; my father was not unkind, but he was irritable and strict . . . Everyone in the house, beginning with my mother, was afraid of him. I remember, when he sent for us, my brother and I used to cross ourselves and hope no one was looking. My father would sometimes caress me, but even in his arms I would freeze. My brother broke with him when he grew up – you may have heard about that – I'll never forget that dreadful day . . . I remained an obedient daughter to my father to the very end – he called me his solace, his Antigone . . . he became blind during his last years . . . , but no matter how tender and gentle he was with me, it didn't efface the memories of childhood – I was terrified of him – a blind old man! In his presence I never felt free – perhaps traces of those early fears, that long imprisonment, still haven't completely disappeared. I know that at first I seem – how shall I put it? – cold, isn't that it? – but I see that I'm telling you about myself instead of talking to you about Kolya. I only wanted to say to you that I know from my own personal experience how much better it is for a child to grow up in freedom . . . Now, I don't suppose *you* were ever much held down as a child?

BELYAEV: How shall I put it, madam . . . nobody took away my freedom – nobody took any notice of me.

NATALYA PETROVNA *shyly:* But your father . . . didn't he . . .

BELYAEV: Oh, he had no time for that, madam, he was always away, going from one neighbour's house to another – that was his business . . . well, perhaps not exactly business . . . but it was through these people, so to speak, that he earned his keep . . . by rendering certain services to them.

NATALYA PETROVNA: So nobody looked after you – after your education?

BELYAEV: No, frankly, nobody – nobody at all. And I daresay – it shows . . . I am only too well aware of my shortcomings.

NATALYA PETROVNA: Perhaps . . . but on the other hand . . . *Stops, and continues with a certain embarrassment.* By the way, Aleksei Nikolaich, was it you singing in the garden yesterday?

BELYAEV: When, ma'am?

NATALYA PETROVNA: Last evening, near the pond – it was you?

BELYAEV: Yes, madam. *Hurriedly.* I never thought – it's so far to the pond – I didn't think it could be heard from here.

NATALYA PETROVNA: Oh, you seem to be apologising . . . but you have a very agreeable musical voice, and you sing beautifully. Have you studied music?

BELYAEV: No, madam, not at all. I sing by ear . . . just simple songs.

NATALYA PETROVNA: You sing them beautifully . . One day I'll ask you . . . not now, only when we get to know each other better – when we become real friends – and we shall be friends, shan't we, Aleksei Nikolaich? I have total confidence in you – all my idle chatter surely shows you that. *She holds out her hand for him to shake: Belyaev takes it uncertainly, and after some perplexity, not knowing what to do with her hand, kisses it. Natalya Petrovna blushes, and takes her hand away. At this moment, Shpigelsky comes in from the hall, stops, and then takes a step backwards. Natalya Petrovna rises quickly. Belyaev also rises.*

NATALYA PETROVNA *embarrassed:* Ah, it's you, Doctor – and we, Aleksei Nikolaich and I *(stops)* – we are here . . . we . . .

SHPIGELSKY *loudly, in an easy-going manner:* The things that go on here, Natalya Petrovna! You can't imagine! In the servants' quarters I asked to see the sick coachman, and lo and behold my patient is sitting up at table, wolfing down *blini* with onion! Try and be a doctor after that, try depending on sickness as an innocent source of income!

NATALYA PETROVNA *with a forced smile:* Yes, indeed. *Belyaev makes as if to leave.* Aleksei Nikolaich, I forgot to tell you . . .

VERA *running in from the hall:* Aleksei Nikolaich, Aleksei Nikolaich. *She sees Natalya Petrovna and stops suddenly.*

NATALYA PETROVNA *somewhat surprised:* What's the matter? What do you want?

VERA *blushing, with lowered eyes, pointing to Belyaev:* They're calling for him.

NATALYA PETROVNA: Who's calling?

VERA: Kolya – I mean, Kolya asked me about the kite . . .

NATALYA PETROVNA: Oh. *In a loud voice to Vera.* On n'entre pas comme cela dans une chambre, cela ne convient pas.[1] *Turning to Shpigelsky.* What time is it, Doctor? Your watch is always right. It must be time for dinner.

SHPIGELSKY: One moment, I am pleased to *(he takes his watch out of his pocket)* inform you that it is now twenty minutes past four o'clock.

NATALYA PETROVNA: You see. It's time. *Goes up to the mirror and arranges her hair; in the meantime Vera whispers something to Belyaev. Both laugh. Natalya Petrovna sees them in the mirror. Shpigelsky gives her sidelong glances.*

BELYAEV *laughing, in a low voice:* No, really?

VERA *nodding her head, also in a low voice:* Yes, yes, really, she did fall off.

NATALYA PETROVNA *with feigned indifference, turns to Vera:* What's that – someone fell?

VERA *in some confusion:* No, madam, Aleksei Nikolaich made a swing – so Nanny took it into her head . . .

NATALYA PETROVNA *without waiting for Vera to finish, to Shpigelsky:* Oh by the way, Shpigelsky, could you come here. *Takes him aside and turns to Vera.* She hasn't hurt herself, has she?

VERA: Oh no, ma'am.

NATALYA PETROVNA: Ye-es . . . but all the same, Aleksei Nikolaich, you shouldn't have . . .

MATVEI *enters from the hall and announces:* Dinner is served, madam.

NATALYA PETROVNA: Oh . . . but where is Arkadi Sergeich? They're going to be late again, he and Mikhailo Aleksandrovich.

MATVEI: They're in the dining-room, madam.

NATALYA PETROVNA: And Mama?

1 You shouldn't come into the room like that, it's not done.

MATVEI: Madam is in the dining-room too.

NATALYA PETROVNA: Oh, let's go then. *Points to Belyaev.* Vera, allez en avant, avec Monsieur.[1]

Matvei goes out, followed by Belyaev and Vera.

SHPIGELSKY *to Natalya Petrovna:* You wanted to say something to me?

NATALYA PETROVNA: Yes, I did, only you see . . . oh, let's talk about it later – about your proposition.

SHPIGELSKY: Ah – about Vera Aleksandrovna?

NATALYA PETROVNA: Yes . . . I'll think about it . . . I'll think it over. *Goes into the hall.*

1 Vera, you go first with Mr Belyaev.

END OF ACT ONE

A garden. On the right and left, under the trees, benches; in front, raspberry bushes. Enter from the right Katya and Matvei. Katya holds a basket.

MATVEI: Well, what's it to be, Katerina Vassilyevna? I mean – it's time, I mean, we got things clear – I do beg you, Miss, to tell me.

KATYA: Matvei Yegorych, Oh! but surely . . .

MATVEI: Katerina Vassilyevna, you know well enough, I mean, the way I feel about you . . . Of course, I'm older than you are, in age I mean to say – there's no denying *that* – that's how it *is*: but I can still stand up for myself, I can, there's plenty of life left in me yet, I don't have to tell you that. What more do you want?

KATYA: Matvei Yegorych, I've a real, deep feeling for you, I'm truly thankful to you, Matvei Yegorych . . . truly, I am, but then . . . I am thinking it would be better to wait a little while.

MATVEI: Wait? What for, Katerina Vassilyevna? You didn't used to talk like that before, if you don't mind my saying, and as for *respect*, you can be sure of that, you can trust me – you'll receive such respect, Katerina Vassilyevna, as nobody could ask for more. And may I say, I don't drink and I've never had a cross word from my masters.

KATYA: Oh dear, Matvei Yegorych, I just don't know what to say.

MATVEI: Katerina Vassilyevna, I've noticed, it's only lately that you've begun to talk like this.

KATYA *blushing slightly:* Why do you say that? How do you mean, 'lately'?

MATVEI: Oh, I don't know . . . only before . . . you . . . are quite different with me.

KATYA *glancing at the wings, hastily:* Look out, the German's coming.

MATVEI *bitterly:* Oh, curse him, the long-nosed stork. We'll have another talk about this. *He goes to the right, Katya wants to go to the raspberry bushes. Enter from the left, Schaaf, with a fishing rod over his shoulder.*

SCHAAF *to Katya:* Vhere? Vhere, Katerine?

KATYA *stopping:* I've been ordered to pick raspberries, Adam Ivanych.

SCHAAF: Rassperr ees goot frukt. You lige rasszper?

KATYA: Yes, I do.

SCHAAF: Ha, ha, ha ... and I ... I alzo. I lov everissing zat you lov. *Seeing she wishes to go.* Oh Katerine vait, a liddle.

KATYA: I haven't time – the housekeeper will be very cross with me.

SCHAAF: Ah, zat's nossing. I too go *(pointing to the fishing rod),* how you zay, fish take. You onterstant, get fish out. You like fish?

KATYA: Yes, sir.

SCHAAF: Ha, ha, ha – and I too, I too. So Katerine, you know vat I vill dell you, in Sherman is a liddle song. *Sings.* '*Kathrinchen, Kathrinchen, wie liebe ich dich so sehr!*' Zat is in Roshian 'Oh Katrynoushka, Katrynoushka, you are pyootiful, I love zee.' *Tries to put his arms around her.*

KATYA: Don't, don't, aren't you ashamed of yourself? – they're coming. *Escapes into the raspberry bushes.*

SCHAAF *his face assumes a severe expression; in a low voice:* Das ist dumm.[1]

Enter from the right Natalya Petrovna, arm in arm with Rakitin.

NATALYA PETROVNA *to Schaaf:* Ah, Adam Ivanych, going fishing?

SCHAAF: Qvite zo, ma'am.

NATALYA PETROVNA: Where is Kolya?

SCHAAF: Mit Lissavet Poktanovna – lesson on fortepiano.

NATALYA PETROVNA: I see. *Glancing around her.* Are you here alone?

SCHAAF: Qvite alone.

NATALYA PETROVNA: You haven't seen Aleksei Nikolaich?

SCHAAF: No, I haf not.

NATALYA PETROVNA *after a silence:* We'll come with you, Adam Ivanych – do you mind? To watch you catch fish?

SCHAAF: I am ferry happy.

RAKITIN *in a low voice to Natalya Petrovna:* Why on earth?

NATALYA PETROVNA *to Rakitin:* Come along, come along, *beau ténébreux*[2]. *All three go to the right.*

KATYA *anxiously pokes her head out from the raspberry bushes:* They've gone. *Comes out, and stops a moment, thoughtfully.* That German! Well I never! *Starts picking raspberries again, humming in a low voice:* 'It's not fire that burns, it's not pitch that boils, it's the restless heart that burns and boils' – Matvei Yegorych is right – *Continues to hum.* 'It burns and boils, my restive heart. Not for father of mine, not for mother of

1 That's stupid.
2 Dark handsome stranger.

mine' – such big raspberries – *Goes on singing.* 'Not for father of mine, not for mother of mine' – oh, the heat, it's so stuffy today. *Continues to sing.* 'Not for father of mine, not for mother of mine, but it boils and it burns, burns for . . .' *Suddenly looks round and is silent, half hides behind the bushes; from the left enter Belyaev and Vera; Belyaev holds a kite in his hand.*

BELYAEV *passing the raspberry bushes, to Katya:* Why have you stopped, Katya? *Sings.* 'Boils and burns for a lovely maiden.'

KATYA: It doesn't go on like that with us.

BELYAEV: How does it go then? *Katya laughs, and doesn't answer.* What are you doing, picking raspberries? Can we have a taste?

KATYA *giving the basket to him:* Take them all.

BELYAEV: No, why take them all? Vera Aleksandrovna, would you like some? *She takes some raspberries from the basket, so does he.* That's enough for me. *Wants to give the basket back to Katya – Katya pushes away his hand.*

KATYA: No, no, take them all, take them.

BELYAEV: No, thank you, Katya. *Gives the basket back to her.* Thank you. *To Vera.* Vera Aleksandrovna, let's sit down on the bench – look at this. *Pointing to the kite.* I must fix the tail; will you help me? *Both go and sit on the bench; Belyaev puts the kite in her hands.* That's right – mind now, hold it straight! *Begins to tie the tail.* What's the matter?

VERA: I can't see you like that.

BELYAEV: What do you want to see me for?

VERA: I mean, I want to see how you tie on the tail.

BELYAEV: Ah, well, wait a moment. *Arranges the kite so that she can see what he is doing.* Katya, why aren't you singing? Do go on. *After a little while, Katya begins again, in a low voice.*

VERA: Tell me, Aleksei Nikolaich, do you sometimes fly kites in Moscow too?

BELYAEV: Oh no, I wouldn't have time for kites in Moscow – hold the string . . . like that. You think we've nothing else to do in Moscow?

VERA: Well . . . what do you do in Moscow?

BELYAEV: What do you mean, what do we do? We study, we listen to the professors.

VERA: What do they teach you?

BELYAEV: Everything.

VERA: You must be a very good student. Better than all the others.

BELYAEV: No, not very good. What do you mean, better than all the others! I'm lazy.

VERA: Why are you lazy?

BELYAEV: Oh, God knows! Born like that, I expect.

VERA *after a silence:* Tell me – have you friends in Moscow?

BELYAEV: Yes, of course . . . oh dear, this string isn't strong enough.

VERA: Do you love them?

BELYAEV: Yes, of course . . . don't you love your friends?

VERA: Friends . . . I have no friends.

BELYAEV: I mean, I meant to say – the girls you know.

VERA *slowly:* Yes.

BELYAEV: Surely you have some you like?

VERA: Yes . . . only I don't know why . . . lately I haven't thought about them much . . . why, I didn't even answer Liza Moshnina, and oh, how she begged me to in her letter.

BELYAEV: What do you mean, you have no friends – and what am I?

VERA *smiling:* Ah . . . that's different. *After a silence.* Aleksei Nikolaich . . .

BELYAEV: What?

VERA: Do you write poetry?

BELYAEV: No, why?

VERA: Oh, nothing. *After a silence.* A girl at my boarding school wrote poetry.

BELYAEV *tightening the knot with his teeth:* Oh, really, and was it any good?

VERA: I don't know – she used to read them to us and we used to cry.

BELYAEV: Why did you cry?

VERA: We felt sorry for her. So, so sorry.

BELYAEV: Did you go to school in Moscow?

VERA: Yes, in Moscow, to Madame Bolus's academy. Natalya Petrovna took me away from there last year.

BELYAEV: Do you love Natalya Petrovna?

VERA: I do – she's so kind, I love her very much.

BELYAEV *with a mocking grin:* You're afraid of her, too, aren't you?

VERA *also grinning:* A little.

BELYAEV *after a silence:* Who sent you to that school?

VERA: Natalya Petrovna's mother – she's dead now. I grew up in her house. I'm an orphan.

BELYAEV *his hands fall:* An orphan? You don't remember your father or your mother?

VERA: No.

BELYAEV: My mother is dead too. We're both orphans. But there's nothing we can do about it. Still, we mustn't let that make us miserable.

VERA: They say that orphans make friends with one another quickly.

BELYAEV *looking into her eyes:* Really? And what do you think?

VERA *looking into his eyes with a smile:* I think they do.

BELYAEV *laughs, and starts working on the kite again:* I'd like to know how long I've been here, in this place?

VERA: Twenty-eight days today.

BELYAEV: What a memory you have! There, the kite is finished. Look, what a beautiful tail! – we must go and fetch Kolya.

KATYA *coming up to them with her basket:* Would you like some more raspberries?

BELYAÉV: No, thank you, Katya. *Katya goes away silently.*

VERA: Kolya is with Lizaveta Bogdanovna.

BELYAEV: What an idea – cooping up a child indoors in this weather.

VERA: Lizaveta Bogdanovna would only have got in our way.

BELYAEV: Oh, I'm not talking about her.

VERA *hastily:* Oh, Kolya couldn't come with us without her. By the way, they said very nice things about you yesterday.

BELYAEV: Really?

VERA: You don't like her?

BELYAEV: Why talk about her – let her take her snuff to her heart's content. Why are you sighing?

VERA *after a silence:* Nothing. How clear the sky is!

BELYAEV: Is that why you are sighing? *Silence.* Perhaps you are bored?

VERA: Bored? No. I don't myself know what makes me sigh . . . no, I'm not bored a bit. On the contrary . . . *After a silence.* I don't know . . . I, I don't think I can be very well today. Yesterday I was going upstairs to get a book – and suddenly on the stairs, can you imagine? I suddenly sat down and burst into tears . . . God knows why. Then after that tears kept coming to my eyes . . . what does it mean? And yet I feel quite happy.

BELYAEV: That's growing up. You're growing. That's what happens. So that's why your eyes looked so swollen last night.

VERA: You noticed?

BELYAEV: Of course.

VERA: You notice everything.

BELYAEV: Well, no . . . not everything.

VERA *thoughtfully:* Aleksei Nikolaich . . .

BELYAEV: What?

VERA *after a silence:* What was it I was going to ask you? I've completely forgotten what I was going to ask.

BELYAEV: Were you thinking about something else?

VERA: No – no . . . Oh yes! I know what it was . . . I think you were telling me that you have a sister?

BELYAEV: I have.

VERA: Tell me, do I look like her?

BELYAEV: Oh no – you are much better looking.

VERA: How is that possible! Your sister . . . I wish I were in her place.

BELYAEV: What? You'd like to be living in our little house?

VERA: That's not what I wanted to say . . . Is your house very small?

BELYAEV: Very. Not like this one.

VERA: What does one need so many rooms for?

BELYAEV: What for? You'll find out in time what all those rooms are for.

VERA: In time . . . when?

BELYAEV: When you have a house of your own.

VERA *pensively:* Do you think so?

BELYAEV: You'll see. *After a silence.* Well, then, Vera Aleksandrovna, should we go and fetch Kolya, d'you think?

VERA: Why don't you call me Verochka?

BELYAEV: And do you think you could . . . you could call me Aleksei?

VERA: Why not? *With a sudden shudder.* Oh!

BELYAEV: What is it?

VERA *in a low voice:* Natalya Petrovna is coming.

BELYAEV *also in a low voice:* Where?

VERA *pointing with her head:* There, coming down the path, with Mikhailo Aleksandrych.

BELYAEV *getting up:* Let's go and fetch Kolya . . . I expect he's finished his lesson by now.

VERA: Yes, let's . . . otherwise . . . I'm afraid she may scold me . . .

Both rise and quickly go to the left. Katya hides in the raspberry bushes again. From the right Natalya Petrovna and Rakitin enter.

NATALYA PETROVNA *stopping:* Isn't that Mr Belyaev walking away with Verochka?

RAKITIN: Yes, indeed it is.

NATALYA PETROVNA: It looks as if they are running away from us.

RAKITIN: Maybe.

NATALYA PETROVNA *after a silence:* I must say, I don't think that Verochka should . . . be alone with a young man in the garden like this . . . Of course she is a child, but still, it's not right . . . I'll speak to her.

RAKITIN: How old is she?

NATALYA PETROVNA: Seventeen! She's seventeen years old . . . It's hot today. I feel tired. Let's sit down. *They sit down on the bench on which Vera and Belyaev had been sitting.* Has Shpigelsky gone?

RAKITIN: Yes.

NATALYA PETROVNA: A pity – you should have made him stay. I wonder what made a man like that become a country doctor . . . he's very entertaining, he makes me laugh.

RAKITIN: It was my impression that you weren't in a laughing mood today.

NATALYA PETROVNA: What made you think that?

RAKITIN: I just did.

NATALYA PETROVNA: Because I'm not in the mood for anything at all emotional today? Yes, I warn you, today nothing in the world could possibly move me. But that doesn't stop me from laughing, on the contrary. Besides, there's something I want to discuss with Shpigelsky.

RAKITIN: And may I be told what that is?

NATALYA PETROVNA: No, you may not. Anyway, you know all that I think and do – it's a great bore.

RAKITIN: You must forgive me . . . I did not mean . . .

NATALYA PETROVNA: I want to have at least one secret from you.

RAKITIN: Oh, really – anyone who heard you talk would think that I knew everything . . .

NATALYA PETROVNA *interrupting him:* And don't you?

RAKITIN: You are pleased to laugh at me.

NATALYA PETROVNA: So you really don't know precisely what goes on inside me? In that case, I can't congratulate you. What? A man watches me from morning till night . . .

RAKITIN: Is that meant to be a reproach?

NATALYA PETROVNA: A reproach? *After a silence.* No, I see now: you aren't very discerning.

RAKITIN: Perhaps not . . . But since I watch you from morning till night, would you allow me to make an observation?

NATALYA PETROVNA: At my expense? Please do.

RAKITIN: You won't be angry with me?

NATALYA PETROVNA: Oh no, I'd quite like to be, but I won't.

RAKITIN: For some time, Natalya Petrovna, you've been in a state of constant irritation, an involuntary inward irritation, as if you were struggling with yourself and didn't know what was happening. Before my visit to the Krinitsyns, I didn't notice it – it all started quite recently. *Natalya Petrovna draws designs on the ground with the tip of her parasol.* Sometimes you sigh so deeply . . . like someone who's tired, terribly tired, and yet somehow cannot get any rest.

NATALYA PETROVNA: And what conclusion do you derive from this, Mr Observer?

RAKITIN: None . . . But it worries me.

NATALYA PETROVNA: I am greatly obliged to you for your concern.

RAKITIN: And besides . . .

NATALYA PETROVNA *with some impatience:* Could we please change the subject. *Silence.*

RAKITIN: You're not going for a drive anywhere today?

NATALYA PETROVNA: No.

RAKITIN: I wonder why not? It's a beautiful day.

NATALYA PETROVNA: Indolence. *Silence.* Tell me . . . you know Bolshintsov, do you not?

RAKITIN: Our neighbour, Afanasi Ivanych?

NATALYA PETROVNA: Yes.

RAKITIN: What an extraordinary question – it was only the day before yesterday that we were playing *préférence* here.

NATALYA PETROVNA: What kind of man is he? I'd like to know.

RAKITIN: Bolshintsov?

NATALYA PETROVNA: Yes, yes, Bolshintsov.

RAKITIN: Well, I must say, I did not expect *that*!

NATALYA PETROVNA *impatiently:* What didn't you expect?

RAKITIN: That you would ever ask me about Bolshintsov – that stupid, fat, heavy man – although I suppose there's nothing positively to be said against him.

NATALYA PETROVNA: He's not as stupid or heavy as you think.

RAKITIN: Maybe. I admit I've not made a careful study of the gentleman.

NATALYA PETROVNA *with irony:* He's not someone you've been observing?

RAKITIN *with a forced smile:* Why, what made you think . . .

NATALYA PETROVNA: I just did! *Silence again.*

RAKITIN: Natalya Petrovna, look how beautiful this dark green oak is against the deep blue of the sky. It's all flooded by the rays of the sun and what overwhelming colours . . . How much indestructible life and power there is in that tree, particularly if you compare it with that young birch . . . which seems all but dissolved in sunshine, its tiny leaves gleam with a kind of liquid glow, as if melting into nothing, and yet it, too, is beautiful.

NATALYA PETROVNA: You know, Rakitin, I noticed this a long time ago . . . You are wonderfully sensitive to the so-called beauties of nature, and talk about them exquisitely . . . very intelligently . . . so exquisitely, so intelligently, that I feel sure nature should be indescribably grateful to you for your beautifully chosen, happy phrases about her; you court nature, like a perfumed marquis on his little red-heeled shoes, pursuing a pretty peasant girl . . . the only trouble is, I sometimes think that nature will never be able to understand or appreciate your subtle language – just as the peasant girl wouldn't understand the courtly compliments of the marquis; nature is simpler, yes, cruder than you suppose – because, thank God, she is healthy . . . Birches don't melt, they don't have fainting fits like ladies with weak nerves.

RAKITIN: *Quelle tirade! Nature* is healthy . . . whereas you imply that I am not?

NATALYA PETROVNA: It's not only you, neither of us is exactly healthy.

RAKITIN: Oh, I know only too well this innocuous way of saying the most wounding things . . . Instead of telling someone straight to his face 'You're a fool, my friend', all you need say, with a winning smile, is: 'We're rather stupid, you know, you and I.'

NATALYA PETROVNA: You're offended! – really, how absurd! I only wanted to say that we're both . . . you don't like the word 'unhealthy' – that we're both getting old, very old.

RAKITIN: Why old? I don't consider myself old.

NATALYA PETROVNA: No, but listen to me: here we are, sitting here at this moment . . . a quarter of an hour ago, two really young creatures may have been sitting on this very bench.

RAKITIN: You mean Belyaev and Verochka? Yes, of course they're younger than we are, but there's only a difference of a few years between us, that's all . . . that does not make us old.

NATALYA PETROVNA: The difference between us and them isn't just one of age.

RAKITIN: Ah, I understand . . . you envy them . . . their naiveté, their freshness, their innocence . . . in other words, their stupidity.

NATALYA PETROVNA: You think so? You really think that they are stupid? I see – everybody seems stupid to you today. No, you don't understand me. Besides . . . stupid? What's wrong with that? What's the use of intelligence if it's not entertaining? There's nothing more depressing than a joyless intellect.

RAKITIN: Hmm. Why can't you be quite straightforward with me – why can't you tell me straight out that I don't amuse you – that's what you really wanted to say . . . why go on about intellect when all you mean is poor old me?

NATALYA PETROVNA: No, you just don't understand. *Katya emerges from the raspberry bushes.* And what have you got there, Katya? Raspberries?

KATYA: Yes, ma'am.

NATALYA PETROVNA: Show me. *Katya goes up to her.* They're beautiful, and so red – but your cheeks are redder still. *Katya smiles and lowers her eyes.* Well, off you go. *Katya leaves.*

RAKITIN: Another young creature of the kind you like so much?

NATALYA PETROVNA: Of course. *Gets up.*

RAKITIN: Where are you going?

NATALYA PETROVNA: First of all I want to see what Verochka is doing . . . it's time she was in . . . And secondly, I confess there's something about our conversation I don't care for. I'd rather not go on with all this talk about nature and youth, at least for a while.

RAKITIN: Perhaps you'd rather walk by yourself?

NATALYA PETROVNA: To tell you the truth, yes. We shall meet soon . . . But we're still friends? *Holds out her hand to him.*

RAKITIN *rising:* Why, yes, of course. *Presses her hand.*

NATALYA PETROVNA: Goodbye. *She opens her parasol and goes off to the left.*

RAKITIN *walks up and down for a while:* What is the matter with her? *After a silence.* A mood, perhaps. A mood? Is it that? I've never seen her like this before. Quite the contrary: I know no woman more even-tempered – what can it be? *Walks up and down, then suddenly stops.* Oh, how funny people are who've only one thought in their heads, one purpose, one thing in their lives . . . like me, for example. What she said was perfectly true: if one has nothing but trivialities to look at from morning till night, one becomes trivial oneself . . . All that's true. But I cannot live without her – her mere presence makes me more than happy; this feeling cannot be called happiness, I belong to her entirely. To give her up would be – I'm not exaggerating – to give up life itself. What's happening to her? What is the meaning of this inner anguish? This involuntary sarcasm? Have I begun to bore her? Hmmm. *Sits.* I've never deceived myself; I know very well the kind of love which she feels for me, but I had hoped that this quiet feeling would in time . . . I had hoped! . . . but do I dare, have I the right, to hope? I admit my situation is rather absurd . . . almost contemptible. *A silence.* But why use such words? She is an honest woman, and I am no Lothario *(with a bitter smile)* – unfortunately. *Rises quickly.* Well, enough . . . enough of all this nonsense. *Walking up and down.* What a beautiful day! *After a silence.* Oh, how cleverly she stung me . . . my 'beautifully chosen phrases' . . . she's very intelligent, particularly when she is in a bad temper. And why this sudden paean of praise to simplicity and innocence? This Russian tutor . . . she often talks to me about him. I must say, I cannot see anything remarkable in him, just a student like any other. But then she . . . no, that's not possible! She's simply in a bad temper, doesn't know what she wants and so she scratches me. After all, children hit their nurses . . . what a flattering comparison. But it's best not to interfere. When this fit of gloom and anxiety passes, she'll be the first to laugh at this lanky creature, this callow youth . . . Not a bad explanation, Mikhailo Aleksandrych, my friend, but is it the *truth*? God only knows. We shall see. After all, this isn't the first time that you've been in this kind of situation, and then you've had to reject all your theories and hypotheses and fold your hands quietly and meekly and wait for the outcome. But in the meanwhile, you must admit that you feel pretty uncomfortable, in fact, quite wretched . . . But then that's your trade. *Looks round.* Ah, here he comes, our young innocent. I haven't had a single real conversation with him yet. Let's find out what he's really like. *Belyaev enters from the left.* Ah, Aleksei Nikolaich, you've been taking the air too?

BELYAEV: Yes, sir.

RAKITIN: I must say, it's not very fresh today – it's fearfully hot, but here under the lime trees, in the shade, it's quite tolerable. *After a silence.* Have you seen Natalya Petrovna?

BELYAEV: I've just met her . . . she's gone to the house with Vera Aleksandrovna.

RAKITIN: Was it you we saw here with Vera Aleksandrovna about half an hour ago?

BELYAEV: Yes, sir, we were taking a walk.

RAKITIN *takes him by the arm:* Well, and how do you like life in the country?

BELYAEV: I love the country; there's only one thing missing: there's no shooting.

RAKITIN: You like shooting?

BELYAEV: I do, sir . . . don't you?

RAKITIN: I? No, I'm no good at it, I'm too lazy.

BELYAEV: I'm lazy too, but not when it comes to walking.

RAKITIN: What form does your laziness take? Perhaps you don't read much?

BELYAEV: No, I love reading, but I'm too lazy for long hours of work, particularly when one has to concentrate on one subject the whole time.

RAKITIN *smiling:* Does that include conversation with ladies, for instance?

BELYAEV: Oh, now you're laughing at me ... Ladies rather frighten me.

RAKITIN *with a certain embarrassment:* What makes you think ... why should I be laughing at you?

BELYAEV: Oh, I don't know ... Anyway, I don't mind. *After a silence.* Do you know where I can get some gunpowder here?

RAKITIN: In the town, I should think – you can buy it there but they call it poppy-seed. Do you want good gunpowder?

BELYAEV: No, just the ordinary stuff. It's not for shooting, I need it for fireworks.

RAKITIN: Ah, you know how to ...

BELYAEV: Yes, I do. I've chosen the place, at the back of the pond. I've heard that it's Natalya Petrovna's birthday in about a week's time, so that would be a good time for it.

RAKITIN: Such a mark of respect from you will give Natalya Petrovna great pleasure ... she likes you, Aleksei Nikolaich, I can tell you that.

BELYAEV: I feel greatly flattered ... By the way, Mikhailo Aleksandrych, I think you subscribe to a periodical, don't you? Would you let me look at it?

RAKITIN: Gladly, with pleasure ... there's some good verse in it.

BELYAEV: I don't much like poetry.

RAKITIN: Why?

BELYAEV: I don't know; comic verse always seems to me rather artificial, and anyhow there isn't a great deal of it. As for the poetry of feeling ... I don't know ... I just don't believe in it, somehow.

RAKITIN: You prefer novels?

BELYAEV: Yes, sir. I like good novels ... but it's critical essays that really grip me.

RAKITIN: Why?

BELYAEV: Because they're written with such warm feeling.

RAKITIN: And you yourself – do you do anything in the way of writing?

BELYAEV: Oh no sir, what's the use of writing if God hasn't given you the talent for it? People would find it ridiculous. Besides, there's something curious – perhaps you could do me a favour and explain it – why do people who seem otherwise perfectly intelligent, when they put pen to paper produce the most terrible rubbish. No, writing is not for me. I only hope that I can understand what others write.

RAKITIN: Let me tell you something, Aleksei Nikolaich: there aren't many young men who have as much common sense as you have.

BELYAEV: Thank you for the compliment. *After a silence.* I've chosen the place for the fireworks at the back of the pond because I know how to make Roman candles which burn on water.

RAKITIN: That must be very beautiful . . . Aleksei Nikolaich, you won't mind my asking you – do you know French?

BELYAEV: No. I did translate Paul de Kock's novel *The Dairymaid of Montfermeil* – maybe you've heard of it? – for fifty roubles in notes; but I don't know a word of French. Imagine, I've translated '*Quatre-vingt-dix*' as four-twenty-ten – I needed the money, you see. But it's a pity. I'd love to know French. It's my damnable laziness again. I'd love to read George Sand in French. And then there's the pronunciation . . . what does one do about *that*? *an, on, en, eun* . . . it's just awful!

RAKITIN: Well, one can manage that, you know.

BELYAEV: Could you please tell me what time it is?

RAKITIN *looks at his watch:* Ten past one.

BELYAEV: Why is Lizaveta Bogdanovna keeping Kolya so long at the piano? He must be dying to get away.

RAKITIN *gently:* But one has to study too, Aleksei Nikolaich.

BELYAEV *with a sigh:* Mikhailo Aleksandrych, *you* shouldn't have to remind me of that, and I ought not to have to hear it. Not everyone, of course, is as bone idle as I am.

RAKITIN: Oh, come, now . . .

BELYAEV: But that's something I really do know.

RAKITIN: And I know the exact opposite. It's quite clear to me that what you think of as a fault in yourself, your naturalness, your freedom, your spontaneity – that is precisely what people find attractive.

BELYAEV: Who, for example?

RAKITIN: Well, Natalya Petrovna, for one.

BELYAEV: Natalya Petrovna? I don't feel in the least free – to use your words – in *her* presence.

RAKITIN: Really?

BELYAEV: Oh, but surely, Mikhailo Aleksandrych, don't you think that education is the most important thing in a man? It's all very well for you to say . . . I don't quite understand you . . . What's that? Was that a corncrake I heard in the garden? *Suddenly stops. Wants to go.*

RAKITIN: Yes, maybe. But where are you off to?

BELYAEV: To get my gun. *Goes towards wings, left; Natalya Petrovna meets him halfway.*

NATALYA PETROVNA *seeing him, suddenly smiles:* Where are you going, Aleksei Nikolaich?

BELYAEV: I'm . . . I'm . . .

RAKITIN: To get his gun . . . He heard a corncrake in the garden.

NATALYA PETROVNA: Oh, please don't shoot in the garden. Let the poor bird live. And besides, you might frighten Grandmama.

BELYAEV: Very good, ma'am.

NATALYA PETROVNA *laughing:* Oh! Aleksei Nikolaich, you should be ashamed of yourself. 'Very good, ma'am'. What sort of words are these? How can you . . . talk to me like that? But wait; Mikhailo Aleksandrych and I are going to undertake your educa-tion . . . Yes, yes . . . he and I have talked about you already . . . more than once . . . I warn you, there's a plot against you. You will let me look after your education, won't you?

BELYAEV: Oh, really . . .

NATALYA PETROVNA: First of all, don't be shy, it doesn't suit you a bit. Yes, we shall look after you. *Pointing to Rakitin.* We're old people, he and I – you're young . . . isn't that so? You'll see it'll all be a great success. You'll look after Kolya, and I . . . we will look after you.

BELYAEV: I shall be most grateful to you.

NATALYA PETROVNA: That's better. What were you talking about here, with Mikhailo Aleksandrych?

RAKITIN *smiling:* He was telling me how he translated a French book – without knowing a word of French.

NATALYA PETROVNA: There you are, we shall teach you French too. By the way, what have you done with your kite?

BELYAEV: I took it back to the house, I didn't think you . . . you liked it much.

NATALYA PETROVNA *with a certain embarrassment:* Why did you think

that? Because Verochka . . . because I took Verochka indoors?
No, that's . . . no, you were quite wrong. *With animation.* I'll tell you
what, Kolya must have finished his lesson by now. Let's fetch him
and Verochka and the kite – would you like that? Then we could
all go to the meadow. Shall we do that?

BELYAEV: With pleasure, Natalya Petrovna.

NATALYA PETROVNA: Splendid. Well, then, let's go, let's go. *Offers
him her arm.* Take my arm, how clumsy you are! Come along, quick!
They both go off rapidly to the left.

RAKITIN *following them with his eyes:* Such life . . . such gaiety . . . I've
never seen such an expression on her face before. What a sudden
transformation! *After a silence.* '*Souvent femme varie*'[1] But I . . . I'm
definitely no use to her today. That's clear. *After a silence.* Well, let's
see what happens next. *Slowly.* Only she can't *(waves his arm about)* . . .
no, it's not possible . . . but that smile, that soft, welcoming,
glowing look . . . Oh, God preserve me from the pangs of jealousy,
especially senseless jealousy. *Suddenly looks round.* Well, well, well
. . . and where have *they* sprung from? *Enter from left Shpigelsky and
Bolshintsov; Rakitin goes to meet them.* How are you, gentlemen? I
confess, Shpigelsky, I didn't expect you today. *Shakes hands with
them.*

SHPIGELSKY: As a matter of fact, I myself, er . . . didn't mean . . .
As a matter of fact, I called on him *(pointing to Bolshintsov)* and he was
already in his carriage coming here. So I turned round and came
back with him.

RAKITIN: Oh well, you are most welcome.

BOLSHINTSOV: I was actually going to . . .

SHPIGELSKY *cutting him short:* The servant told us that everyone was
in the garden . . . There was nobody in the drawing-room.

RAKITIN: Why, didn't you see Natalya Petrovna?

SHPIGELSKY: When?

RAKITIN: Just now.

SHPIGELSKY: No, we didn't come straight from the house.
Afanasi Ivanych wanted to see if there were any mushrooms in the
spinney.

BOLSHINTSOV *with obvious astonishment:* I . . . I . . .

1 'Woman is fickle', after Verdi's celebrated tenor aria in *Rigoletto*, which is adapted
from Victor Hugo's play *Le roi s'amuse*: it is quoted in the novel by Dumas which
Rakitin has been reading aloud.

SHPIGELSKY: Oh, we all know you love browncaps. So Natalya Petrovna has gone back to the house. Well, then we can go back too.

BOLSHINTSOV: Yes, of course.

RAKITIN: She went in to get everybody together for a walk. I think they're planning to fly a kite.

SHPIGELSKY: Admirable. One should be out of doors on a day like this.

RAKITIN: If you'd like to stay here . . . I'll go and tell them you've arrived.

SHPIGELSKY: No, why should you bother . . . no, really, Mikhailo Aleksandrych!

RAKITIN: No, I have to go in anyway.

SHPIGELSKY: Ah well, in that case we won't stop you . . . No standing on ceremony here, you know.

RAKITIN: Goodbye, gentlemen. *Goes to the left.*

SHPIGELSKY: Goodbye. *To Bolshintsov* Well, Afanasi Ivanych . . .

BOLSHINTSOV *interrupting him:* What was all that about mushrooms, Ignati Ilyich? I couldn't make out . . . what mushrooms?

SHPIGELSKY: Oh, so you'd have preferred me to say, would you, that Afanasi Ivanych was much too scared to go straight into the house and wanted to slip in through a side door?

BOLSHINTSOV: That's true . . . but all this about mushrooms . . . I don't know, maybe I'm wrong.

SHPIGELSKY: You certainly are wrong, my dear fellow. I'll tell you what *you'd* better be thinking about: here we both are . . . in this place, as you desired. Be careful now, and don't fall flat on your face.

BOLSHINTSOV: Yes, Ignati Ilyich, you did . . . you did tell me, that is . . . I should like to know definitely what the answer is . . .

SHPIGELSKY: Look, my dear sir, Afanasi Ivanych! Your place is over ten miles away, and you've asked me this question at least three times every mile . . . isn't that enough? Now, listen to me – only this is the last time I am doing this for you. What Natalya Petrovna said to me was 'I . . .'

BOLSHINTSOV *nodding his head:* Yes.

SHPIGELSKY *irritably:* 'Yes' . . . what do you mean, 'yes'? – I haven't told you anything yet . . . She said, 'I don't know Mr Bolshintsov at all well, but he seems to me a good man; on the other hand, I've not the slightest intention of putting any pressure on Verochka, therefore let him call on us: if he wins –'

BOLSHINTSOV: 'Wins'? Did she say 'wins'?

SHPIGELSKY: '. . . if he wins favour in her eyes, Anna Semyonovna and I won't stand in the way.'

BOLSHINTSOV: 'Won't stand in the way'? Is that what she said? 'Won't stand in the way'?

SHPIGELSKY: 'Yes, yes, yes. What a funny fellow you are to be sure. 'We won't stand in the way of their happiness.'

BOLSHINTSOV: Hmm.

SHPIGELSKY: 'Their happiness', yes. You must realise, Afanasi Ivanych, what your task is . . . you now have to convince Vera Aleksandrovna herself that marriage to you really will make her happy; you must win her affection.

BOLSHINTSOV *blinking:* Yes, yes, win – exactly so; I agree.

SHPIGELSKY: You absolutely insisted on my bringing you here today . . . well, let's see how you act now.

BOLSHINTSOV: Act? Yes, yes, one must act, one must win, that's it. There's just one thing, Ignati Ilyich, since you're my best friend, I must tell you about one shortcoming of mine: you said that I wanted you to bring me here today.

SHPIGELSKY: 'Wanted'? . . . you insisted, you kept pestering me.

BOLSHINTSOV: Well yes . . . that's true. But it's like this: at home . . . as it were . . . at home I felt ready for anything, but now I'm overcome by nerves.

SHPIGELSKY: Why are you so nervous?

BOLSHINTSOV *looking at him with a worried look:* It's a bit risky.

SHPIGELSKY: Whaa-at?

BOLSHINTSOV: Risky, it's a tremendous risk, Ignati Ilyich, I must confess to you, since . . .

SHPIGELSKY *interrupting him:* Because I'm your best friend . . . I know, I know . . . go on.

BOLSHINTSOV: Yes, yes – that's right. I must confess, Ignati Ilyich, that I . . . I've not had much to do with ladies – that is, I mean, the female sex; I must be quite frank with you, Ignati Ilyich, it's simply I've no idea what one can talk about with persons of the female sex . . . and quite alone . . . face to face, particularly with a young woman.

SHPIGELSKY: You do astonish me. I don't know what one *can't* talk about with a person of the female sex, particularly with a young woman, and particularly when one is alone with her.

BOLSHINTSOV: Well, of course, you ... How can I compete with you. That's why I need your advice about this – so to speak – this situation. They do say that in matters of this sort it's the first step that is so very hard. So couldn't you think of a suitable word or two, some nice opening – then I'll carry on myself? I'll manage somehow after that.

SHPIGELSKY: I'm not going to suggest suitable phrases to you, Afanasi Ivanych, because those words wouldn't be of the slightest use to you ... But I can give you a piece of advice if you like.

BOLSHINTSOV: Oh do, please, my dear sir, I'd be most grateful ... as for gratitude ... You know what I mean ...

SHPIGELSKY: Do stop – I'm not bargaining with you.

BOLSHINTSOV *lowering his voice:* About that, that troika – that's all in order, you know.

SHPIGELSKY: Do stop, I tell you. Look, Afanasi Ivanych, you are – no question about it – a most excellent man in every respect; *(Bolshintsov bows slightly)* you are a man of excellent character.

BOLSHINTSOV: You're too kind.

SHPIGELSKY: Moreover, you own, I think, three hundred souls?

BOLSHINTSOV: Three hundred and twenty.

SHPIGELSKY: Mortgaged?

BOLSHINTSOV: I don't owe a penny to anyone.

SHPIGELSKY: You see! I told you you were a most wonderful man, and a marvellous suitor. And you say yourself that you've had little to do with the ladies ...

BOLSHINTSOV *with a sigh:* That's so: I have, you might say, Ignati Ilyich, avoided the female sex since childhood.

SHPIGELSKY: Well, there you are. That isn't a vice in a husband, on the contrary; but still, on certain occasions – for example, when declaring one's love for the first time – one has to be able to say *something* – wouldn't you agree?

BOLSHINTSOV: I agree with you entirely.

SHPIGELSKY: Otherwise Vera Aleksandrovna might simply think that you weren't feeling well. Besides, your appearance – not that there's anything at all wrong with it – isn't exactly what one would call striking, the kind that immediately attracts the eye – and that's needed nowadays.

BOLSHINTSOV *with a sigh:* Nowadays . . .

SHPIGELSKY: That's the kind of thing young ladies like these days. Yes, and of course – there's your age . . . In short, it's not just amiability that attracts people. So you'd better not be thinking about pretty speeches. That won't be much of a support. But you have a far more dependable and solid asset – your character, my dear Afanasi Ivanych, that and your three hundred and twenty souls. In your case, I should simply say to Vera Aleksandrovna . . .

BOLSHINTSOV: When we're alone?

SHPIGELSKY: Oh, absolutely, only when you're alone: 'Vera Aleksandrovna,' *by the movement of Bolshintsov's lips it is clear that he is repeating in a whisper every one of Shpigelsky's words* 'I love you and ask for your hand. I am a kind man, simple, quiet and not poor. With me you would have complete freedom; and I shall do everything possible to please you. Couldn't you make enquiries about me, and couldn't you pay me a little more attention than you have so far? You can give me your answer, whatever it may be, whenever you like. I am prepared to wait, why, I should even consider it a pleasure.'

BOLSHINTSOV *repeating the last word aloud:* '. . . a pleasure' – yes, yes, that's it, you're right. Only one thing, Ignati Ilyich, I think you used the word 'quiet' . . . as though to say – that I was a quiet sort of man.

SHPIGELSKY: Well, and aren't you a quiet sort of man?

BOLSHINTSOV: Ye-e-es: but all the same, all the same, I'm not sure . . . is that the kind of word one should use . . . wouldn't it be better, Ignati Ilyich, to say, for instance . . .

SHPIGELSKY: For instance what?

BOLSHINTSOV: For instance – for instance – *after a silence* – oh well, perhaps one could say 'quiet' . . . very well . . .

SHPIGELSKY: Look here, Afanasi Ivanych, you listen to me: the simpler your words, the fewer flowers of speech you use, the better for you, believe me. The main thing is, don't insist, don't insist, Afanasi Ivanych; Vera Aleksandrovna is still very young; you might scare her. Give her time to think about your proposition. Oh, and another thing . . . I nearly forgot; but you did say that I might offer you advice . . . You tend to say, my dear Afanasi

Ivanych, words like 'hardichoke' and ''oof' ... well, yes, of course, one can say that ... why not ... but the words 'artichoke' and 'hoof' are rather more usual; they're more the kind of thing that people usually say. Because once, I remember, I heard you call a hospitable squire 'Bonvoyou' – what you said was something like 'What a Bonvoyou he is'! That's another good sort of word, of course, but, unfortunately it doesn't mean anything. I'm not, you know, too good at French words myself, but I do know this much. Don't try and use big words and I'll guarantee success. *Looking round.* Ah, here they all are, all coming this way. *Bolshintsov wants to leave.* Where are you going? After mushrooms again? *Bolshintsov smiles, blushes and stays.* The main thing is, not to lose your nerve!

BOLSHINTSOV *hastily:* Vera Aleksandrovna, she doesn't know anything yet, does she?

SHPIGELSKY: Of course not.

BOLSHINTSOV: Well, I'm relying on you. *He blows his nose.*

Natalya Petrovna, Vera, Belyaev, with the kite and Kolya, enter from the left, followed by Rakitin and Lizaveta Bogdanovna.

NATALYA PETROVNA *in a very good mood, to Bolshintsov and Shpigelsky:* How do you do, gentlemen, good afternoon, Shpigelsky, I didn't expect you today, but I'm always glad to see you. How do you do, Afanasi Ivanych. *Bolshintsov bows in a slightly embarrassed manner.*

SHPIGELSKY *to Natalya Petrovna, pointing to Bolshintsov:* This distinguished gentleman insisted on bringing me here.

NATALYA PETROVNA *laughing:* That's very good of him ... but do you have to be forced to come here?

SHPIGELSKY: Oh, goodness ... but I was here only this morning – I ... no, really ...

NATALYA PETROVNA: Ah, you're caught – I've caught you, *Monsieur le diplomate.*

SHPIGELSKY: I am delighted, Natalya Petrovna, to see you in such a cheerful mood, if I may say so.

NATALYA PETROVNA: Oh, you think it's worth remarking upon it – does it happen so seldom?

SHPIGELSKY: Oh good gracious, no, no ... of course ...

NATALYA PETROVNA: *Monsieur le diplomate,* you're getting more and more entangled.

KOLYA *who all the time has been moving impatiently, near Belyaev and Vera:* Please, Mama, when are we going to fly the kite?

NATALYA PETROVNA: Whenever you want to. Aleksei Nikolaich, and you Verochka, let's go to the meadow. *Turning to the others.* Gentlemen, I doubt whether this is going to amuse you much. Lizaveta Bogdanovna, and you, Rakitin, we'll leave our good Afanasi Ivanych in your hands.

RAKITIN: But Natalya Petrovna, why do you think that we would not enjoy it?

NATALYA PETROVNA: Oh, all you clever people, you'll think it rather childish . . . Still, it is as you like, we won't stop you from following us. *To Belyaev and Vera.* Let's go. *Natalya, Vera, Belyaev and Kolya move off to the right.*

SHPIGELSKY *looking with a certain surprise at Rakitin, addresses Bolshintsov:* Afanasi Ivanych, won't you offer you arm to Lizaveta Bogdanovna?

BOLSHINTSOV *hastily:* Oh, with pleasure. *Offers his arm to Lizaveta Bogdanovna.*

SHPIGELSKY *to Rakitin:* And I'll come with you, if I may, Mikhailo Aleksandrych. *Takes him by the arm.* Just look at them tripping down the avenue. Even though we may be clever people, let's go and watch them fly their kite. Afanasi Ivanych, won't you go ahead?

BOLSHINTSOV *walking with Lizaveta Bogdanovna:* The weather today, is, is most, one might say, is . . . is, very pleasurable.

LIZAVETA BOGDANOVNA *mincing:* Oh yes, very.

SHPIGELSKY *to Rakitin:* Mikhailo Aleksandrych, there's something that I should like to discuss with you. *Rakitin suddenly laughs.* Why, what is it?

RAKITIN: Oh, nothing . . . I think it's funny that we should be bringing up the rear.

SHPIGELSKY: The vanguard, you know, can turn into the rearguard very easily . . . It only takes a change of direction. *All move off to the right.*

END OF ACT TWO

ACT THREE

Décor as Act One. Rakitin and Shpigelsky enter from the hall.

SHPIGELSKY: Well then, Mikhailo Aleksandrych, I need your help, would you do me a favour?

RAKITIN: How can I help you, Ignati Ilyich?

SHPIGELSKY: How? Come, Mikhailo Aleksandrych: put yourself in my place. Actually, of course, all this hasn't much to do with me: I acted, you know, out of a simple desire to please . . . my kind heart will be the end of me.

RAKITIN *laughing:* Oh, I don't think you're in mortal danger yet.

SHPIGELSKY *also laughing:* Who can tell? But I've got myself into a distinctly awkward situation. I brought Bolshintsov here at Natalya Petrovna's request. I conveyed the answer to him with her permission. And now, one side is annoyed with me as if I'd done something stupid, while the other side – Bolshintsov – gives me no peace. They avoid *him*, and won't speak to *me*.

RAKITIN: Whatever possessed you, Ignati Ilyich, to embark on the whole business? After all, between ourselves, Bolshintsov is nothing but an ass.

SHPIGELSKY: Between ourselves indeed! It's not exactly news! But since when did only intelligent people get married? Whatever else, you really cannot forbid fools to marry. You say that I started it . . . Not at all. What happened was this: a friend asks me to say a kind word on his behalf. Well, what am I to do? Refuse him? I'm a kind man, I don't know how to say no. I carry out my friend's request. The answer? 'It's most kind of you; thank you so much; but please do not trouble yourself any further.' I quite understand and do no more. After which I am suddenly instructed from this very quarter – and encouraged, I may say – to reopen the subject . . . I obey. Result: indignation. In what way am I to blame?

RAKITIN: Who says you are to blame? . . . There's only one thing surprises me – why do you keep going on about it so?

SHPIGELSKY: Why . . . why? The fellow gives me no rest.

RAKITIN: Oh, come, that's not –

SHPIGELSKY: Besides, he's an old friend of mine.

RAKITIN *smiles sceptically:* Oh, ah, well – that's another matter.

SHPIGELSKY *also smiling:* Oh, well, I'll be frank with you. I can't take you in. Well then, yes . . . he promised me . . . my trace-horse has gone lame, so well, he – he did promise me –

RAKITIN: Another one?

SHPIGELSKY: No, I must admit – all three – an entire troika.

RAKITIN: You might have said that before!

SHPIGELSKY *vivaciously:* Oh, but please don't think . . . I should never in the world have agreed to act as a go-between in this affair, it's absolutely against my nature *(Rakitin smiles),* if I didn't know Bolshintsov to be an entirely honourable man . . . As a matter of fact, there's only one thing I want now: a definite answer — yes or no.

RAKITIN: Oh, it's gone as far as that, has it?

SHPIGELSKY: What are you thinking of? It's not marriage we're talking about, only permission to come here, to pay visits . . .

RAKITIN: But who could possibly forbid that?

SHPIGELSKY: Oh, you really are . . . *forbid*! Of course anybody else might . . . But Bolshintsov is a timid man, a pure innocent from before the Fall; he's a child, a babe in arms; he has very little self-confidence; he needs encouragement. Besides, his intentions are wholly honourable.

RAKITIN: And his horses are good, too.

SHPIGELSKY: Yes, his horses *are* good. *Takes a pinch of snuff, and offers some to Rakitin.* Won't you?

RAKITIN: No, thank you.

SHPIGELSKY: Yes, that's how it is, Mikhailo Aleksandrych – you see, I don't want to deceive you. Why should I? It's all clear and open, open as the palm of my hand. He's a man of good principles, well-off, quiet . . . If he'll do, well and good. If not, they ought to say so.

RAKITIN: Well, if that's so, it all seems fine. But what am I supposed to do? I don't see how I can help.

SHPIGELSKY: Come, Mikhailo Aleksandrych, we all know perfectly well that Natalya Petrovna has great respect for you, and sometimes even follows your advice . . . Mikhailo Aleksandrych *(puts his arm round him),* be a good friend, put in a tiny little word for me!

RAKITIN: And you think he'll make a good husband for Verochka?

SHPIGELSKY *with a serious air:* I'm quite sure of it. You don't believe it

... but you'll see. The main thing in marriage – you know that yourself – is to have a solid character: and Bolshintsov is solid as a rock. *Looking round.* Ah, here is Natalya Petrovna herself coming towards us – dearest friend, I beg and beseech you, my dearest friend, do this for me: be a father to me, be good to me. Two chestnuts and the bay between the shafts! Do this for me, please.

RAKITIN *smiling:* Very well, very well.

SHPIGELSKY: Don't forget, I rely on you. *Escapes into the hall.*

RAKITIN *looking after his retreating form:* What a cunning rogue this doctor is! Verochka ... and Bolshintsov! And yet, why not? There are worse marriages. I'll do what he asks; the rest is no business of mine. *Turns round.*

NATALYA PETROVNA *coming out of the study and seeing him, stops; then irresolutely:* Oh ... it's you ... I thought you were in the garden.

RAKITIN: You don't seem pleased.

NATALYA PETROVNA *interrupting him:* Oh do stop! *Moves to the front of the stage.* Are you alone?

RAKITIN: Shpigelsky has just gone.

NATALYA PETROVNA *with a slight frown:* Our local Talleyrand ... What has he been telling you? Is he still hanging about?

RAKITIN: The local Talleyrand, as you call him, is evidently not in favour with you today, yet only yesterday ...

NATALYA PETROVNA: He's funny ... he's amusing, but he meddles in other people's business, and that's rather unpleasant. Moreover, in spite of that very obsequious manner, he is exceedingly impudent and importunate ... he is a great cynic.

RAKITIN *going up to her:* This is not how you talked about him yesterday.

NATALYA PETROVNA: Maybe. *With some animation.* Well, anyway, what was he talking to you about?

RAKITIN: He talked to me about Bolshintsov.

NATALYA PETROVNA: Oh, that silly man.

RAKITIN: That is not how you talked about him either, yesterday.

NATALYA PETROVNA *with a forced smile:* Yesterday is not today.

RAKITIN: That's so for everybody else ... but evidently not for me.

NATALYA PETROVNA *lowering her eyes:* What do you mean?

RAKITIN: For me today is the same as yesterday.

NATALYA PETROVNA *holding out her hand to him:* I understand your reproach, but you are wrong: yesterday I would not have admitted my guilt about the way I behaved to you. *Rakitin wants to stop her.* No, don't contradict me . . . I know and you know what I want to say . . . but today I am ready to admit it. I've thought over many things today . . . believe me, Michel, however silly my thoughts sometimes are, whatever I say, whatever I do, there's no one I depend on as I do on you. *Lowering her voice.* There is no one . . . I *love* no one as I love you . . . You don't believe me? *A short silence.*

RAKITIN: I believe you . . . but you somehow look depressed today . . . What is it?

NATALYA PETROVNA *doesn't listen to him, and continues:* I am now convinced of one thing, Rakitin; one can never answer for oneself, one can't guarantee anything. We often don't understand our past . . . So how can we possibly answer for the future! One can't bind the future in chains of iron!

RAKITIN: That's true.

NATALYA PETROVNA *after a long silence:* Listen, I want to be quite frank with you. It may be that I shall cause you some pain . . . but I know that if I kept the truth from you, that would hurt you even more. I confess, Michel, this young student . . . This Belyaev, has made quite a strong impression on me.

RAKITIN *in a low voice:* I knew that.

NATALYA PETROVNA: Ah, you've noticed it? Since when?

RAKITIN: Since yesterday.

NATALYA PETROVNA: Oh.

RAKITIN: Do you remember, two days ago I spoke to you about the change in you . . . I didn't know then what could have caused it. But yesterday after our last talk . . . In the meadow . . . if only you could have seen yourself! I didn't recognise you, it was as if you were someone else. You laughed, you jumped up and down, you romped like a little girl, your eyes were shining, your cheeks were burning, and you gazed at him with such wonder and interest, such trust, such joy, and your smile . . . *Glancing at her.* Even now the mere recollection of it makes your face light up. *Turns away.*

NATALYA PETROVNA: No, Rakitin, for God's sake don't turn away from me . . . Listen, why exaggerate? This man has infected me with his youth, that's all. I have never been young myself, Michel, since my childhood until now . . . You know my life, you know it all . . . I'm not used to this, it has gone to my head like wine, but I know that it will pass as quickly as it came . . . It's not worth talking about. *After a silence.* Only don't turn away from me, don't take your hand away . . . help me . . .

RAKITIN *sotto voce:* Help you . . . cruel words. *Loudly.* Natalya Petrovna, you don't know yourself what is happening to you; you seem convinced that it's not worth talking about, and you beg for help . . . Clearly you must feel you need it.

NATALYA PETROVNA: Well . . . yes . . . I appeal to you as a friend.

RAKITIN *bitterly:* Yes, ma'am . . . Natalya Petrovna, I'll do my best to deserve your trust in me . . . but would you allow me to collect myself a little . . .

NATALYA PETROVNA: Collect yourself? Why, are you afraid of some . . . unpleasantness? Has something changed?

RAKITIN *bitterly:* Oh, no! Everything is exactly as it was.

NATALYA PETROVNA: Why, what are you thinking, Michel? Surely you don't imagine . . .

RAKITIN: I don't imagine anything.

NATALYA PETROVNA: Oh, well, if you despise me to such a degree . . .

RAKITIN: Do stop, for God's sake! We'd better talk about Bolshintsov. The doctor is waiting for a reply about Verochka, you know.

NATALYA PETROVNA *sadly:* Are you angry with me?

RAKITIN: I? Oh, no, but I am sorry for you.

NATALYA PETROVNA: Really? Now that does annoy me. Michel, aren't you ashamed? *Rakitin remains silent; she shrugs her shoulders and continues with irritation.* You say the doctor is waiting for an answer? And who asked him to interfere?

RAKITIN: He assured me that you yourself . . .

NATALYA PETROVNA *interrupting him:* Maybe, maybe . . . Although I don't think I said anything definite to him. Besides, I can change my mind. And anyway, for goodness sake, what *does* it matter? Shpigelsky's got a finger in all sorts of pies, he can't expect all his schemes to come off.

RAKITIN: He only wants to know what answer . . .

NATALYA PETROVNA: What answer . . . *After a silence.* Enough, Michel! Give me your hand . . . why this air of indifference, this cold politeness? What have I done that is so wrong? Think a moment: is it really my fault? I came to you hoping for good advice, I didn't hesitate for a moment, I never thought of hiding anything from you — while you . . . I see now I shouldn't have been so frank with you . . . Why, it would never have entered my head . . . You suspected nothing . . . You've deceived me. And now, God knows what you are thinking.

RAKITIN: I? Really, how can you!

NATALYA PETROVNA: Give me your hand. *He doesn't move; she continues, slightly offended.* Are you actually turning your back on me? Well then, so much the worse for you. However, I don't blame you. *Bitterly.* — You are jealous.

RAKITIN: I have no right to be jealous, Natalya Petrovna . . . What *are* you saying?

NATALYA PETROVNA *after a silence:* As you will. About Bolshintsov: I haven't spoken about it to Verochka yet.

RAKITIN: I could send her to you *now.*

NATALYA PETROVNA: Why now? However, just as you please.

RAKITIN *going to the door of the study:* Do you wish me to send her here?

NATALYA PETROVNA: Michel, for the last time . . . You have just said that you are sorry for me . . . Is that how sorry you are? Can you really . . .

RAKITIN *coldly:* Am I to send her?

NATALYA PETROVNA *with annoyance:* Yes.

Rakitin goes to the study: Natalya Petrovna remains motionless for a time, then sits down, takes a book from the table, opens it, lets it drop in her lap. He too! What *is* all this? He — he too — and I relied on him. And Arkadi? Goodness, I haven't even thought of him. *Drawing herself up.* I see that it's time I put a stop to all this. *Vera enters from the study.* Yes, it really is time.

VERA *timidly:* You sent for me, Natalya Petrovna?

NATALYA PETROVNA *looking round quickly:* Ah, Verochka, yes I did ask you to come.

VERA *going up to her:* Aren't you well?

NATALYA PETROVNA: I? Yes, I'm well — why?

VERA: I thought . . .

NATALYA PETROVNA: No, it's nothing — I'm a little hot — that's all. Sit down. *Vera sits down.* Listen, Vera, you are not busy at the moment, are you?

VERA: No, ma'am.

NATALYA PETROVNA: I ask you that because I must have a talk with you . . . a serious talk. You see, my darling, until now you were still a child; but you are seventeen; you're a sensible girl . . .

It's time you thought about your future. You know that I love you like a daughter; my house will always be your home . . . but in other people's eyes you are an orphan, you're not rich, there may come a time when you will be tired of always having to live with strangers. Listen, do you want to be a mistress, complete mistress, in your own house?

VERA *slowly:* I don't understand you, Natalya Petrovna.

NATALYA PETROVNA *after a silence:* Your hand is being asked for in marriage. *Vera looks at Natalya Petrovna with amazement.* You didn't expect this: I confess it seems a little odd to me too. You are still so young . . . I needn't tell you that I haven't the least intention of putting any pressure on you . . . I think it is a little early for you to marry, but I considered it my duty to tell you . . . *Vera suddenly covers her face with her hands.* Vera . . . what is this, you're crying? *Takes her by the hand.* You're trembling all over . . . surely you are not afraid of me, Vera?

VERA *dully:* I'm in your power, Natalya Petrovna.

NATALYA PETROVNA *takes Vera's hands from her face:* Vera, aren't you ashamed to be crying? Aren't you ashamed of saying that you're in my power? What do you think I am? I am talking to you as if you were my daughter, and you . . . *Vera kisses her hands.* Aha! So you're in my power? Very well then, please laugh at once . . . That is an order. *Vera smiles through her tears.* That's better. *Natalya Petrovna puts an arm around her and draws her closer.* Vera, my child, can't you treat me as if I were your mother, or, no, better still, imagine that I am your elder sister, and do let's have a talk about all these wonderful things . . . would you like to?

VERA: Very well, ma'am.

NATALYA PETROVNA: Well then, listen . . . come closer. That's it. First of all, since you are my sister, I don't need to tell you that you are at home here, completely at home. Such pretty little eyes are at home everywhere. Consequently, the idea that you might be a burden to anyone, that anyone could possibly want to get rid of you, couldn't conceivably enter your head . . . Do you hear? But then, one fine day, your sister comes to you and says 'Imagine, Vera, you have a suitor . . .' Well, what would you answer? That you are still very young, that you aren't thinking of marriage?

VERA: Yes, ma'am.

NATALYA PETROVNA: Don't say ma'am to me – one doesn't say that to a sister, does one?

VERA *smiling:* Well then . . . yes.

NATALYA PETROVNA: Your sister will agree with you, the suitor will be refused, and that'll be the end of it. But if the suitor happens to be a good man, quite well off, and if he's ready to wait, if he only asks permission to see you occasionally, in the hope that you'll get to like him in time . . .

VERA: Who is this suitor?

NATALYA PETROVNA: Ah, you'd like to know – you can't guess?

VERA: No.

NATALYA PETROVNA: You've seen him today. *Vera blushes.* It's true, he's not very handsome, and not very young . . . Bolshintsov.

VERA: Afanasi Ivanych?

NATALYA PETROVNA: Yes . . . Afanasi Ivanych.

VERA *after looking for some time at Natalya Petrovna, suddenly begins to laugh, then stops:* You're not joking?

NATALYA PETROVNA *smiling:* No . . . but, I can see, that's that as far as Bolshintsov is concerned. If you had cried when you heard his name there might have been some hope for him, but you laughed: now there's nothing for him to do but take himself off, go home.

VERA: I'm sorry . . . but I confess I never expected . . . Do people still marry at his age?

NATALYA PETROVNA: Why, how old do you think he is? He is not fifty, he's in the prime of life.

VERA: Maybe . . . but he has such a peculiar face . . .

NATALYA PETROVNA: Don't let's talk about him. He's dead and buried. Forget him. Of course, it's only natural: someone like Bolshintsov couldn't possibly appeal to a girl of your age . . . You want to marry for love, not convenience, don't you?

VERA: Yes, Natalya Petrovna, but you . . . Didn't you marry Arkadi Sergeich for love?

NATALYA PETROVNA *after a silence:* Yes, for love, of course. *After another silence, and squeezing Vera's hand.* Yes, Vera . . . I just said you were very young . . . but young people are right . . . *Vera lowers her eyes.* Well then, it's settled, Bolshintsov is dismissed. I must admit that I myself shouldn't really have liked to see his puffy old face next to your fresh little one, though he's actually a very good man. Now you see how wrong you were to be afraid of me? How quickly we've settled it all! *Reproachfully.* Really, you've treated me as if I were your benefactress! You know how I hate that word.

VERA *embracing her:* Forgive me, Natalya Petrovna.

NATALYA PETROVNA: That's better. Are you sure you are not afraid of me?

VERA: No, I love you, I'm not afraid of you.

NATALYA PETROVNA: Thank you, my dear. Now we're great friends and we won't have any secrets from each other. Well now, if I asked you, Verochka, whisper it in my ear, is it only because Bolshintsov is so much older than you, and no beauty, that you don't want to marry him?

VERA: But isn't that enough, Natalya Petrovna?

NATALYA PETROVNA: Yes, of course, but is there no other reason?

VERA: I don't know him at all . . .

NATALYA PETROVNA: True, but you're not answering my question.

VERA: There is no other reason.

NATALYA PETROVNA: Really? In that case my advice to you is to think it over. I realise that to be in love with Bolshintsov might not be easy . . . but, I repeat, he is a good man. Now if you were in love with someone else . . . that would be a different matter. But your heart hasn't spoken to you yet?

VERA *timidly:* How do you mean, ma'am?

NATALYA PETROVNA: You don't love anyone else?

VERA: I love you . . . Kolya, I love Anna Semyonovna too.

NATALYA PETROVNA: No, I'm not talking about that kind of love, you don't understand me . . . I mean, for instance, among all the young men whom you might have seen here, or in other people's houses, wasn't there anyone you found attractive?

VERA: No, ma'am . . . I've liked some, but . . .

NATALYA PETROVNA: I noticed, for instance, that at the Krinitsyns' party you danced three times with that tall officer . . . What was his name?

VERA: An officer?

NATALYA PETROVNA: Yes, the man with the large moustache.

VERA: Oh, that man! . . . no, I didn't like him.

NATALYA PETROVNA: Well, and Shalansky?

VERA: Shalansky is a nice man; but he . . . I don't think he's interested in me.

NATALYA PETROVNA: Oh, why?

VERA: He . . . I believe he thinks more about Liza Velskaya.

NATALYA PETROVNA *glancing at her:* Ah . . . you noticed that? *Silence.* Well, and Rakitin?

VERA: I like Mikhailo Aleksandrovich very much.

NATALYA PETROVNA: Yes, like a brother. Well, and Belyaev?

VERA *blushing:* Aleksei Nikolaich? I like Aleksei Nikolaich.

NATALYA PETROVNA *watching Vera:* Yes, he is a nice man. But he's so shy with everybody . . .

VERA *innocently:* No, ma'am, he's not shy with me.

NATALYA PETROVNA: Oh?

VERA: He talks to me, ma'am. Perhaps you think so . . . because he's frightened of you. He hasn't got to know you yet.

NATALYA PETROVNA: And how do you know that he is frightened of me?

VERA: He told me so.

NATALYA PETROVNA: Ah, he told you so . . . So he talks more openly to you than to others?

VERA: I don't know how he is with other people, . . . but with me . . . it may be because we're both orphans. Besides, he looks on me as a child.

NATALYA PETROVNA: Do you think so? As a matter of fact I like him too, very much – he must have a kind heart.

VERA: Oh, very kind, ma'am. If only you knew . . . everybody in the house loves him. He's so sweet, he talks to everybody, he's ready to help anybody. The day before yesterday he carried an old beggar woman from the high road to the hospital in his arms. He picked a flower for me once, from a high, over-hanging rock – I almost closed my eyes I was so terrified; I thought he'd fall and hurt himself . . . But he is so agile! You could see for yourself in the meadow yesterday how agile he is!

NATALYA PETROVNA: Yes, that's true.

VERA: Do you remember when he was running after the kite, how he jumped over the ditch? That's nothing to him.

NATALYA PETROVNA: Did he really pick a flower for you from a dangerous spot? He is obviously very fond of you.

VERA *after a silence:* He's always cheerful . . . always in a good mood . . .

NATALYA PETROVNA: I find that strange. Why, when he's with me . . .

VERA *interrupting:* But I tell you, it's because he doesn't know you. But wait, I'll tell him . . . I'll tell him that there's no reason to be afraid of you – isn't that so? – that you're so kind . . .

NATALYA PETROVNA *with a forced laugh:* Thank you very much.

VERA: You'll see . . . And he does listen to me, even though I am younger than he is.

NATALYA PETROVNA: Oh, I had no idea you were such friends . . . But Vera, do watch out, do be careful. He is, of course, an excellent young man . . . But you know, at your age . . . it won't quite do. People might think . . . I did say this to you, do you remember, yesterday, in the garden? *Vera lowers her eyes.* On the other hand, I don't want to stand in the way of your inclinations, I've too much confidence, both in you and in him . . . But all the same . . . Don't be cross with me, my darling, for being so pedantic . . . We old people are always boring the young with our sermons. However, I've no need to say all this: you like him, and that's all there is to it?

VERA *timidly raising her eyes:* He . . .

NATALYA PETROVNA: That same old look again! That's not the way one looks at a sister. Vera, listen, come a little closer. *Caressing her.* Supposing your sister, your real sister, whispered in your ear 'Verochka, are you really not in love with anybody, no?' What would you answer her? *Vera glances uncertainly at her.* These little eyes want to say something to me. *Vera suddenly presses her face against Natalya Petrovna's breast. Natalya Petrovna goes pale, and after a silence continues.* Are you in love? Tell me, are you in love?

VERA *without lifting her head:* Oh, I don't know myself what's the matter with me . . .

NATALYA PETROVNA: Poor little thing – you're in love . . . *Vera presses herself closer to Natalya Petrovna's bosom.* You *are* in love . . . and he, Vera, *he?*

VERA *still without raising her head:* What do you want me to tell you . . . I don't know . . . Maybe . . . I don't know, I don't know . . . *Natalya Petrovna shudders and remains motionless. Vera lifts her head and suddenly notices an odd expression on her face.* Natalya Petrovna, what's the matter?

NATALYA PETROVNA *recovering herself:* The matter with me? . . .
Nothing . . . What? . . . Nothing.

VERA: You are so pale, Natalya Petrovna, what is it? Would you
like me to . . . Shall I ring? *Gets up.*

NATALYA PETROVNA: No, no . . . don't ring . . . it's nothing . . .
it'll pass. There now, it's over.

VERA: May I at least get someone to come?

NATALYA PETROVNA: No, certainly not – I . . . I want to be alone.
Leave me, do you hear? We'll talk about this later. Off you go.

VERA: But you're not angry with me, Natalya Petrovna?

NATALYA PETROVNA: Angry, I? What about? Of course not, on
the contrary, I'm grateful to you for your trust . . . Only leave me
now, please.

VERA *wants to take her hand, but Natalya Petrovna turns away as if she hadn't
noticed Vera's movements; Vera with tears in her eyes:* Natalya Petrovna . . .

NATALYA PETROVNA: Leave me, please leave me. *Vera goes slowly to
the study. Natalya Petrovna remains motionless for a while.* Now it's all quite
clear . . . These children love one another . . . *She stops and passes her
hand over her face.* Well? So much the better . . . God give them
happiness! *Laughing.* And I, I imagined . . . *Stops again.* It certainly
didn't take long for her to come out with her secret . . . I confess I
had no idea . . . I must say this news astonished me . . . Yet wait,
it's not all over yet. God . . . what am I saying? What's happened
to me? I don't recognise myself. What have I come to? *Pause.* What
am I doing? Marrying off a poor young girl . . . to an old man! . . .
I managed to slip the doctor into the situation . . . he guesses . . .
drops hints. Arkadi, Rakitin . . . and I . . . *She shivers, and suddenly lifts
her head.* Good God, what is it? I, jealous of Vera . . . I . . . I'm in
love with him, is that it? *Pauses.* Do you still doubt it? You're in
love, you wretched woman! How this happened . . . I don't know;
it's as if I'd been poisoned by someone . . . everything's destroyed,
scattered, gone . . . he's frightened of me . . . they're all afraid of
me. What could he see in me? . . . How could he want a creature
like me? He's young, and she's young. And I! *Bitterly.* How could he
begin to know what I really am? They're both idiots . . . as Rakitin
says – oh, how I hate that know-all! And Arkadi – my good,
trusting Arkadi! Oh God, Oh God! I wish I were dead. *Rises.* I
think I'm going out of my mind. But why exaggerate? Well . . . I
am astounded . . . Strange, this is the first time . . . I . . . yes . . . this

is the first time it's happened, I'm in love for the first time in my life. *She sits down.* He must go away. Yes. And Rakitin too. It's time I pulled myself together. I allowed myself to take one step, and this is the result, this is what I have come to. What was it about him that attracted me? *Becomes thoughtful.* Oh, this is it – this terrible feeling . . . Arkadi! Yes, I'll fall into his arms, I'll beg him to forgive me, protect me, save me. He . . . no one else? All the rest are strangers to me, and must remain so . . . But is there . . . is there no other way out? This little girl . . . she's a child. She might have made a mistake. They're nothing but children at play . . . Why should I assume . . . I'll have it out with him, I'll ask him. *Reproachfully.* What! You are still hoping? You still want to hope? And what am I hoping for? Oh God, don't make me despise myself! *Drops her head into her hands. Rakitin comes in from the study, looking pale and worried.*

RAKITIN *going up to Natalya Petrovna:* Natalya Petrovna . . . *She doesn't stir; to himself.* What can have happened between her and Vera? *Aloud.* Natalya Petrovna . . .

NATALYA PETROVNA *lifting her head:* Who is it? Oh, it's you.

RAKITIN: Vera Aleksandrovna told me that you were not well . . . I . . .

NATALYA PETROVNA *looking away:* I'm perfectly well . . . What made her think . . .

RAKITIN: No, Natalya Petrovna, you are not well – you should see yourself.

NATALYA PETROVNA: No, perhaps I'm not, but what's it got to do with you? What do you want? What have you come for?

RAKITIN *with feeling:* I will tell you why I came. I came to ask you to forgive me. Half an hour ago I was unspeakably stupid and rude to you . . . Forgive me . . . You see, Natalya Petrovna, however modest a man's wishes and . . . hopes may be . . . it's difficult for him not to forget himself if only, perhaps for a moment, when these hopes are suddenly snatched from him; but now I've returned to my senses, I've understood my position! I realise what I'm guilty of. There's only one thing I crave for . . . your forgiveness. *He sits down gently next to her.* Look at me . . . don't you turn away from me too. I am with you again, your old Rakitin, your friend, a man who asks for nothing, only to be allowed to serve you . . . to use your phrase, to serve you as a support . . . Don't lose your trust in me, make what use of me you like, and forget that I ever . . . forget everything that may have offended you.

NATALYA PETROVNA *who has been looking fixedly at the floor:* Yes, yes . . . *Stopping.* Oh, I am sorry, Rakitin, I'm afraid I didn't hear a word you were saying.

RAKITIN *sadly:* I said . . . I asked you to forgive me, Natalya Petrovna. I asked you whether you would allow me to remain your friend.

NATALYA PETROVNA *slowly turning towards him and putting both her hands on his shoulders:* Rakitin, tell me – what is the matter with me?

RAKITIN *after a silence:* You are in love.

NATALYA PETROVNA *slowly repeating after him:* I'm in love. But that is madness, Rakitin. It's not possible; can things happen so suddenly? . . . You say I'm in love . . . *She stops.*

RAKITIN: Yes, poor lady, you're in love. Don't deceive yourself.

NATALYA PETROVNA *not looking at him:* What can I do now?

RAKITIN: I'm prepared to tell you, Natalya Petrovna, but only if you'll promise . . .

NATALYA PETROVNA *interrupting him, still not looking at him:* You know this young girl, Vera, loves him . . . They're in love with each other.

RAKITIN: If so, that's one more reason . . .

NATALYA PETROVNA *interrupting him again:* I've suspected this for a long time, but she has confessed it to me herself . . . just now.

RAKITIN *in a low voice, as if talking to himself:* Poor woman!

NATALYA PETROVNA *passing her hand over her face:* And now . . . time I came to my senses. I think you wanted to say something to me . . . for heaven's sake, Rakitin, tell me what to do . . .

RAKITIN: I'm ready to advise you, Natalya Petrovna, but only on one condition.

NATALYA PETROVNA: And that is . . . ?

RAKITIN: Promise me that you won't suspect my motives. Tell me that you believe that my desire to help you is absolutely disinterested; and you must help me, too: your confidence in me will give me strength – otherwise you'd better allow me to say nothing.

NATALYA PETROVNA: Go on, go on.

RAKITIN: You don't doubt me?

NATALYA PETROVNA: Go on.

RAKITIN: Well, then, listen to me: he must go away. *Natalya Petrovna looks at him in silence.* Yes, he must go away. I'm not going to talk to you about . . . your husband . . . your duty. In my mouth such words . . . are out of place . . . But these children love one another . . . you've just told me so yourself; now imagine yourself caught between them . . . this would destroy you!

NATALYA PETROVNA: He must go away . . . *After a silence.* And you, will you stay?

RAKITIN *embarrassed:* I? . . . I? . . . *After a silence.* I must go away too. For your peace of mind, for your happiness, for Verochka's happiness . . . he . . . and I . . . we must both go away for ever.

NATALYA PETROVNA: Rakitin . . . I've sunk so low that I . . . I was almost ready to marry off this poor young girl — an orphan, entrusted to me by her mother — to marry her off to a stupid, ridiculous old man . . . I couldn't do it, Rakitin; the words died on my lips when she simply laughed at my suggestion . . . Yet I enlisted the doctor's help, I let him smile at me in that knowing way, I let him smile, pay me compliments, drop hints . . . Oh, I feel that I'm on the edge of an abyss . . . save me!

RAKITIN: Natalya Petrovna, you see that I was right . . . *She is silent; he continues quickly.* He must go away . . . we must both go away . . . nothing else can save you.

NATALYA PETROVNA *gloomily:* And after that, what will there be left for me to live for?

RAKITIN: Good God, has it come to that . . . Natalya Petrovna, you'll recover, believe me . . . All this will pass. How can you say, what is there to live for?

NATALYA PETROVNA: Yes, yes, why go on living when everyone is deserting me?

RAKITIN: But . . . your family . . . *Natalya Petrovna lowers her eyes.* Listen, if you want me to, I *could* remain for a few days after he's gone . . . in order, in order to . . .

NATALYA PETROVNA *sombrely:* Ah, I understand — you're counting on habit, on old friendship . . . You're hoping that I shall come to my senses, that I shall return to you; isn't that it? I understand.

RAKITIN *flushing:* Natalya Petrovna, why do you insult me?

NATALYA PETROVNA *bitterly:* I understand you . . . but you deceive yourself.

RAKITIN: What? After your promises? When it was only for you, for you alone, for your happiness, for your position in society, when all I wanted . . .

NATALYA PETROVNA: Really? Since when have you been so deeply concerned about that? Why haven't you ever mentioned it to me before?

RAKITIN *rising:* Natalya Petrovna, I'm leaving this house today, and you will never see me again . . . *Wants to go.*

NATALYA PETROVNA *holding her hand out to him:* Michel, forgive me; I don't know what I'm saying . . . you see the state I'm in. Forgive me.

RAKITIN *quickly returns to her and takes her hands:* Natalya Petrovna . . .

NATALYA PETROVNA: Oh Michel, I'm utterly miserable . . . *Leans on his shoulder and presses her handkerchief to her eyes.* Help me, I'm lost without you.

At this moment, the door of the hall opens and Islayev and Anna Semyonovna enter.

ISLAYEV *loudly:* That always was my opinion . . . *Stops in amazement at the sight of Rakitin and Natalya Petrovna. Natalya Petrovna looks round, and quickly leaves; Rakitin remains, deeply embarrassed.* What does this mean? What *is* all this?

RAKITIN: Oh . . . nothing . . . nothing at all . . . there's . . .

ISLAYEV: Natalya Petrovna is not unwell, is she?

RAKITIN: No . . . but . . .

ISLAYEV: Why did she suddenly run away? What have the two of you been talking about? She seemed to be crying . . . You were trying to comfort her . . . What *is* all this?

RAKITIN: Nothing, I assure you.

ANNA SEMYONOVNA: What do you mean 'nothing', Mikhailo Aleksandrych? *After a silence.* I'll go and see. *Wants to enter the study.*

RAKITIN *stopping her:* No, I beg you, you'd better leave her in peace just now.

ISLAYEV: What does all this mean? Can't you tell me?

RAKITIN: Nothing at all, I swear to you . . . I really do promise to explain all this to you both, today. I give you my word. But if you have the slightest trust in me, please don't ask me any questions now . . . And don't disturb Natalya Petrovna.

ISLAYEV: Very well . . . but it's very odd. Nothing like this has ever happened to Natasha before. This is something unusual.

ANNA SEMYONOVNA: The thing I can't understand is – what made Natasha cry? And why did she run away? What are we – strangers?

RAKITIN: What *are* you saying! How can you talk like that! But actually I must admit we didn't finish our conversation . . . I must ask you . . . both of you – to leave us alone for a while.

ISLAYEV: Oh, really! So there is some secret between you?

RAKITIN: Yes, there is, but you'll be told what it is.

ISLAYEV *after a little thought:* Come, Mama . . . let's leave them. Let them finish their mysterious conversation.

ANNA SEMYONOVNA: Oh, but . . .

ISLAYEV: Do come, please come. You heard him, he's promised to explain.

RAKITIN: You can rest assured . . .

ISLAYEV *coldly:* Oh, I'm not worried at all. *To Anna Semyonovna.* Let's go. *They leave.*

RAKITIN *watches them go, then goes up to the door of the study:* Natalya Petrovna . . . Natalya Petrovna . . . come back, I beg you.

NATALYA PETROVNA *comes in from the study. She is very pale:* What did they say?

RAKITIN: Nothing – don't worry . . . They were certainly rather surprised. Your husband thought you weren't well . . . he noticed that you were upset . . . Sit down; you can hardly stand . . . *Natalya Petrovna sits.* I told him . . . I asked him not to disturb you . . . to leave us alone.

NATALYA PETROVNA: And he agreed?

RAKITIN: Yes. I admit I had to promise him that I'd explain it all tomorrow . . . Why did you go away?

NATALYA PETROVNA *bitterly:* Why! . . . But what are you going to tell him?

RAKITIN: I . . . I'll think of something. But that isn't the problem at the moment . . . We must make use of this respite. You do realise that it can't go on like this . . . you're in no state to go through this kind of thing again . . . it's unworthy of you . . . indeed, I myself . . . but that's not the point. If only you remain firm, I'll manage; listen, surely you agree with me . . .

NATALYA PETROVNA: What about?

RAKITIN: About the need . . . for our departure? You do agree? Because if you do, there's no reason for delay. If you'll permit me, I'll talk to Belyaev . . . He's an honourable man, he will understand.

NATALYA PETROVNA: You want to talk to him? You? But what can you say to him?

RAKITIN *embarrassed:* I . . .

NATALYA PETROVNA *after a silence:* Rakitin, listen to me. Don't you think that we're both quite mad? . . . I became frightened, and I frightened you, and perhaps all about nothing at all.

RAKITIN: How do you mean?

NATALYA PETROVNA: No, really . . . what are we doing? A little while ago we were so quiet, so peaceful in this house . . . And suddenly . . . God knows what began to happen! Honestly, we've all gone off our heads. Enough! It's time we stopped this silly nonsense. We must go back to the old life . . . You won't have to explain anything to Arkadi; I'll tell him myself about all these children's games, and we'll have a good laugh about them, both of us. I don't need an intermediary between myself and my husband!

RAKITIN: Natalya Petrovna, now you terrify me. You're smiling and you are as pale as death . . . Don't you remember what you yourself said to me only a quarter of an hour ago?

NATALYA PETROVNA: Oh, lots of things happen! But I see what it is now . . . You are creating this storm yourself . . . so that at least you won't sink alone.

RAKITIN: Again, again, suspicion – more reproaches, Natalya Petrovna . . . how can you . . . You are tormenting me. Or do you regret that you have been so open with me?

NATALYA PETROVNA: I regret nothing.

RAKITIN: Then what do you want me to understand?

NATALYA PETROVNA *with animation:* Rakitin, if you say a single word about me, or from me, to Belyaev, I shall never forgive you.

RAKITIN: Ah, that's how it is! . . . You need not worry, Natalya Petrovna. Not only will I say nothing to Mr Belyaev, I shan't even say goodbye to him when I leave this house. I've no intention of thrusting my services where they are not wanted.

NATALYA PETROVNA *with some embarrassment:* Oh, perhaps you think that I have changed my mind about . . . about his going?

RAKITIN: I think nothing.

NATALYA PETROVNA: On the contrary, I'm so convinced about the need you've spoken of, of his going away, that I propose to dismiss him myself. *After a silence.* Yes! I shall dismiss him myself.

RAKITIN: You?

NATALYA PETROVNA: Yes, I. Now. May I ask you to send him to me.

RAKITIN: What, at this very moment?

NATALYA PETROVNA: Yes, now. Do it, Rakitin, please. You see, I am perfectly calm. No one will disturb me now, so this is the moment . . . I should be very grateful if you did this. There are some questions I want to ask him.

RAKITIN: But he won't tell you anything, I assure you. He told me himself that he doesn't feel at ease with you.

NATALYA PETROVNA *suspiciously:* Oh, so you've been talking to him about me? *Rakitin shrugs his shoulders.* Oh, I'm sorry, Michel, forgive me, and send him here to me. You'll see, I'll tell him to go and it'll all be over. Over and forgotten, like a bad dream. Please tell him to come here. I must have a final talk with him. You'll be pleased with me. Do ask him.

RAKITIN *who hasn't taken his eyes off her all this time – speaking coldly and gloomily:* Very well, your wish will be fulfilled. *Goes to the door of the hall.*

NATALYA PETROVNA *looking after him:* I'm most grateful, Michel.

RAKITIN *turning round:* You might at least spare me your thanks. *Quickly goes through the door.*

NATALYA PETROVNA *alone, after a silence:* He's an honourable man . . . but did I really ever love him? *Gets up.* He is right, Belyaev must go. But how can I tell him that? I only want to know whether he really finds this girl attractive. But perhaps it's all nonsense. But why did I feel so agitated . . . And why all these outpourings? Well, there's nothing to be done about that. I'd like to know what he's going to say to me. But he must go away . . . he must . . . he must. He may not want to answer me . . . he's afraid of me, of course . . . Well then, so much the better, there won't be much to talk about . . . *Puts her hand to her forehead.* I have a headache. Shall I put it off until tomorrow? Perhaps I should. Today I keep feeling that I am being watched all the time . . . what *have* I come to! No, better do it now, once and for all . . . One last effort, and I am free!

. . . Yes, yes! It's peace and freedom that I long for. *Belyaev comes in from the hall.* Here he is . . .

BELYAEV *going up to Natalya Petrovna:* Natalya Petrovna, Mikhailo Aleksandrych said that you wished to see me . . .

NATALYA PETROVNA *with a certain effort:* Yes, that is so . . . I must . . . get things clear.

BELYAEV: Get things clear?

NATALYA PETROVNA *not looking at him:* Yes . . . get an explanation. *After a silence.* I must tell you, Aleksei Nikolaich, that I . . . I am not pleased with you.

BELYAEV: May I know the reason?

NATALYA PETROVNA: You must hear me out . . . I . . . I really don't know how to begin. However, I must explain that my dissatisfaction is not caused by anything . . . you have failed to do . . . on the contrary, I was pleased by the way you've looked after Kolya.

BELYAEV: Then what can it be?

NATALYA PETROVNA *glancing at him:* There is no need to be alarmed . . . what you have done is not so very grave. You are young: you've probably never stayed in other people's houses. You couldn't have foreseen . . .

BELYAEV: But, Natalya Petrovna . . .

NATALYA PETROVNA: You want to know what this is all about? I understand your impatience. Well then, I must tell you that Verochka *(glancing at him)*, Verochka has told me everything.

BELYAEV *astonished:* Vera Aleksandrovna? What was there for Vera Aleksandrovna to tell? What's it all to do with me?

NATALYA PETROVNA: Do you really not know what it is that she told me? You can't guess?

BELYAEV: I . . . I've not the slightest idea.

NATALYA PETROVNA: In that case, you must forgive me. If you really haven't any notion, I must ask you to forgive me. I thought . . . But may I tell you that I do not believe you. I understand what makes you say this . . . I respect your discretion.

BELYAEV: I don't begin to understand, Natalya Petrovna.

NATALYA PETROVNA: Really? Do you expect me to believe that you never noticed that child's, Vera's, feeling for you?

BELYAEV: Vera Aleksandrovna's feelings for me? I simply don't know what to say . . . I really don't. It seems to me that I've behaved towards Vera Aleksandrovna exactly as . . .

NATALYA PETROVNA: As towards everyone else, isn't that so? *After a brief silence.* However that may be, whether you really don't know or are pretending that you don't, the point is that the girl is in love with you. She admitted it to me herself. Now I'm asking you, as an honourable man, what do you propose to do?

BELYAEV *with embarrassment:* What do I propose to do?

NATALYA PETROVNA *crossing her arms:* Yes.

BELYAEV: All this is so unexpected, Natalya Petrovna.

NATALYA PETROVNA *after a silence:* Aleksei Nikolaich, I see . . . that I've not managed this at all well. You don't understand me. You think that I'm annoyed with you . . . But I . . . I'm only . . . a little upset. And this is quite natural. Don't be so agitated . . . Let's sit down. *Both sit down.* I'll be frank with you, Aleksei Nikolaich, and you too must show me a little more trust. You really mustn't be quite so distant with me. Vera loves you . . . of course, that is not your fault, I'll assume that it's no fault of yours . . . but you see, Aleksei Nikolaich, she's an orphan. She's my ward: I am responsible for her, for her future, for her happiness. She is still young, and I feel sure that the sentiment which you have inspired in her may soon pass . . . at her age love doesn't always last. But you must realise that it was my duty to warn you. All the same, playing with fire is dangerous . . . I don't doubt that now that you know what she feels for you, you'll behave differently, you'll avoid meetings or walks in the garden . . . Isn't that so? I can rely on you . . . I should have been afraid of speaking so frankly to someone else.

BELYAEV: Natalya Petrovna, believe me, I appreciate . . .

NATALYA PETROVNA: I've told you that I have complete confidence in you . . . Anyhow, all this will remain a secret between us.

BELYAEV: I must confess to you, Natalya Petrovna, that everything you've just said to me seems to me utterly strange . . . Of course, I shouldn't dare disbelieve you, but . . .

NATALYA PETROVNA: Listen, Aleksei Nikolaich, everything I've said to you just now . . . I said on the assumption that on your part there's nothing . . . *Interrupts herself.* Because if that were not so . . . of course I don't know you at all well, but I know you well enough to have no reason for opposing your wishes. You are not rich . . . but you are young, you have a future, and when two human beings love one another . . . I tell you again that I considered it my duty to warn you, as a man of honour, about the consequences of your friendship with Vera, but if, of course, you . . .

BELYAEV *puzzled:* I really do not know, Natalya Petrovna, what you are trying to tell me.

NATALYA PETROVNA *quickly:* Oh, believe me, I'm not demanding a confession from you, there's no need for that . . . your behaviour makes things clear enough . . . *Glancing at him.* However, I must tell you that Vera was under the impression that you were not wholly indifferent to her.

BELYAEV *after a silence, gets up:* Natalya Petrovna, I see it now. I cannot remain in your house.

NATALYA PETROVNA *flaring up:* You might have waited for me to tell you that myself. *Gets up.*

BELYAEV: You have been frank with me . . . May I be equally frank with you. I do not love Vera Aleksandrovna, at least, I don't love her in the sense you mean . . .

NATALYA PETROVNA: But I did . . . *She stops.*

BELYAEV: And if Vera Aleksandrovna likes me, if she thinks, to use your words, that I too am not indifferent to her, I don't wish to deceive her. I shall tell her everything myself, tell her the whole truth. But you yourself understand that after what you've said to me, Natalya Petrovna, it would be difficult for me to stay here: my position would be too embarrassing. I'm not going to start telling you how painful it will be for me to leave your house . . . but there is nothing else I can do. I shall always think of you with gratitude . . . So would you allow me to go now . . . I shall have the honour of taking my leave of you properly later.

NATALYA PETROVNA *with feigned indifference:* Just as you wish, but I confess I didn't expect . . . that wasn't my purpose in talking to you as I have . . . I only wanted to warn you. Vera is still a child . . . Perhaps I've made too much of it all. I don't see any necessity for you to go. However, it's as you wish.

BELYAEV: Natalya Petrovna . . . I do assure you, it's really quite impossible for me to stay.

NATALYA PETROVNA: You find it quite easy, I see, to say goodbye to us all.

BELYAEV: No, Natalya Petrovna, not easy.

NATALYA PETROVNA: I am not in the habit of trying to keep people against their will ... But I confess that I find this very disagreeable.

BELYAEV *after a certain indecision:* Natalya Petrovna ... I don't want to cause you the least annoyance ... I'll stay.

NATALYA PETROVNA *suspiciously:* Oh, *(after a silence)* I didn't expect you to change your mind so quickly ... I am grateful to you, but ... I must think about this. Perhaps you are right, perhaps it would be better for you to go. I'll think about it and let you know ... May I leave you in a state of uncertainty until this evening?

BELYAEV: I am prepared to wait as long as you like. *Bows and makes as if to leave.*

NATALYA PETROVNA: You promise me ...

BELYAEV *stopping:* What, ma'am?

NATALYA PETROVNA: You said you wanted to talk about this to Vera ... I am not sure that would be quite proper. However, I shall inform you of my decision. I'm beginning to think it might really be better for you to go away. Good day. *Belyaev bows again and goes to the hall. Natalya Petrovna follows him with her eyes.* Oh what a relief! He is not in love with her. *She walks up and down the room.* So, instead of getting rid of him, I've kept him here myself? He's staying ... But what am I going to say to Rakitin? What have I done? *After a silence.* What right had I to tell people about this poor young girl's love? Oh God! First I wormed a confession out of her ... a half confession, and then, ruthlessly, brutally, I myself ... *Covers her face with her hands.* Perhaps he was beginning to care for her ... what right had I to crush that budding flower, to trample it underfoot ... But wait, have I really crushed it? Perhaps he's deceived me ... After all, I wanted to deceive him ... Oh no! he's too honourable for that ... He's not like me! Why was I so frantic? Why did I pour it all out at once? *Sighing.* Well, lots of things happen ... if I could have foreseen ... oh, how I prevaricated, how I lied to him ... And he! How freely, how fearlessly he talked ... I could have gone down on my knees before him – he really *is* a man! I didn't know him before ... He must go away. If he stays ... I feel I shall go too far, I shall lose all my self-respect ... he must go or I am lost! I shall write him a note before he's had time to see Vera ... He must go! *Goes quickly to the study.*

END OF ACT THREE

ACT FOUR

Centre front – large empty hallway. The walls are bare, the stone floor is uneven; six whitewashed, peeling pillars, three on either side, support the ceiling. On the left, two open windows and a door into the garden. On the right, a door to a corridor which leads to the main building; centre back, an iron door to the storeroom. Under the first pillar on the right is a green garden bench; in one corner, several spades, watering cans and pots. It is evening. The red rays of the sun fall on the floor through the windows.

KATYA *comes out of the door on the right, quickly goes up to the window, looks out at the garden for some time:* No. Can't see him. Can't see him anywhere. They said he'd gone to the greenhouse. He doesn't seem to have come out of there. Well, I'll wait till he passes. He can't help but come this way . . . *Sighs, leans against the window.* They say he's going away. *Sighs again.* What will we do without him . . . poor young lady! How she begged and begged me . . . Well, why shouldn't I do something for her? Let him have a good last talk with her. The *heat* today! but I think I felt a drop of rain. *Glances out of the window again and suddenly draws back.* Oh my! If it isn't this way that they're coming . . . It *is.* Oh lord . . . *Makes as if to run away, but before she can reach the door of the corridor Shpigelsky comes in from the garden with Lizaveta Bogdanovna. Katya hides behind a pillar.*

SHPIGELSKY *shaking the rain off his hat:* We can wait here until it's over. The rain won't last long.

LIZAVETA BOGDANOVNA: Yes, we might.

SHPIGELSKY *looking round:* What is this building – a storeroom, is it?

LIZAVETA BOGDANOVNA *pointing to the iron door:* No, the storeroom is over there. This room, so they say, was built on by Arkadi Sergeich's father when he returned from foreign parts.

SHPIGELSKY: Ah, I see what it is: Venice, that's what it is. *Sits down on a bench.* Let's sit down. *Lizaveta Bogdanovna sits.* Don't you agree, Lizaveta Bogdanovna, that it started to rain at a very unsuitable moment? It interrupted our intimate conversation at a most sensitive point.

LIZAVETA BOGDANOVNA *lowering her eyes:* Ignati Ilyich . . .

SHPIGELSKY: But nobody prevents us from beginning again . . . By the way, did you say that Anna Semyonovna was in a bad mood today?

LIZAVETA BOGDANOVNA: Yes, she was. She even had her meal in her room.

SHPIGELSKY: Dear me, how very terrible!

LIZAVETA BOGDANOVNA: This morning she found Natalya Petrovna in tears . . . Mikhailo Aleksandrych was there . . . of course, he's almost one of the family, but still . . . However, Mikhailo Aleksandrych promised to explain everything.

SHPIGELSKY: I see. Well, in that case, she really hasn't any cause for worry. In my opinion, Mikhailo Aleksandrych never was any danger, and now less than ever.

LIZAVETA BOGDANOVNA: Why do you say that?

SHPIGELSKY: Because. He talks a bit too well. Some people come out in a rash, but these know-alls, they work it all off with their tongues, just by talking. Don't ever be afraid of chatterboxes, Lizaveta Bogdanovna, they're not dangerous. The dangerous ones are the silent ones, with a lot of temperament, a little bit mad, with huge backs to their heads, those really *are*.

LIZAVETA BOGDANOVNA *after a silence:* Tell me, is Natalya Petrovna really unwell?

SHPIGELSKY: She's every bit as well as you or I.

LIZAVETA BOGDANOVNA: She did not eat anything at dinner.

SHPIGELSKY: Being ill is not the only cause of loss of appetite.

LIZAVETA BOGDANOVNA: Did you dine with Bolshintsov?

SHPIGELSKY: Yes, I did . . . I went over to see him. And I swear I returned only because of you.

LIZAVETA BOGDANOVNA: Oh come, come now. I'll tell you something, Ignati Ilyich, Natalya Petrovna is cross with you about something . . . she wasn't very complimentary about you at table.

SHPIGELSKY: Really? Ladies don't like it when people like me have eyes to see. You're supposed to do what they want, to help them — and then pretend you don't understand what they're at. That's what they're like. However, we'll have to see what happens. And Rakitin — he's a bit down in the mouth, too, I imagine?

LIZAVETA BOGDANOVNA: Yes, he doesn't seem to be himself either today.

SHPIGELSKY: Hmm. And Vera Aleksandrovna? Belyaev?

LIZAVETA BOGDANOVNA: They're all, the whole lot of them, in a difficult mood today. I simply can't make out what's the matter with them all.

SHPIGELSKY: The more you know, the older you grow, Lizaveta Bogdanovna. Anyway, forget about them. Let's talk about our own affairs. I see it's still raining a bit . . . would you like to?

LIZAVETA BOGDANOVNA *lowering her eyes in a mincing manner:* Are you asking me something, Ignati Ilyich?

SHPIGELSKY: Come, Lizaveta Bogdanovna, what is the point of all this acting, all this coy fluttering of eyelids, may I ask? After all, we aren't exactly young, you and I. These affectations, these soft airs and sighs – it's all slightly absurd at our age. Let's talk this over quietly, in a businesslike manner, as befits our years. Well, then, the question is this: we like each other . . . at least, I am assuming that you like *me*.

LIZAVETA BOGDANOVNA *slightly mincing:* Ignati Ilyich, really . . .

SHPIGELSKY: Yes, yes, of course. I daresay that, as a woman, you are entitled to do a bit of . . . *(gestures with his hand)* oh, all this kind of stuff. But it's clear that we like each other. And we are very well matched in other respects too. Of course I must make it clear that I am not well-born – but then, you're not exactly of high birth either. I'm not rich – if I were, I shouldn't have to . . . *Gives a little laugh.* But I have a very decent practice, and not all my patients die; you say you have fifteen thousand in cash. That's not at all bad, I must say. Besides, I imagine that you're pretty tired of being a governess forever, and all that endless looking after the old woman, always partnering her at *préférence* and having to say 'yes' constantly to anything she says – that can't be very amusing either. As far as I'm concerned, it isn't that I'm tired of bachelor existence, but I'm getting older, yes, and my cooks rob me; so it all seems to fit very nicely, don't you think? But there's one difficulty, Lizaveta Bogdanovna: we don't know each other at all, or rather, to be precise, you don't know me . . . I know *you*, I know your character: I wouldn't say that you've got no faults. Being a spinster has turned you a little sour – but I don't think that matters much. A wife is like wax in the hands of a good husband. But I should like you to know me too before we're married. Otherwise, you might start complaining afterwards . . . I don't want to deceive you.

LIZAVETA BOGDANOVNA *with dignity:* Oh but, Ignati Ilyich, I think I, too, have had plenty of opportunity of knowing what you are like.

SHPIGELSKY: You? Oh, come . . . that's not the kind of thing women know. I'm sure you think that I have a cheerful character, full of fun – isn't that so?

LIZAVETA BOGDANOVNA: I've always thought that you were a most amiable man.

SHPIGELSKY: There you are. You see how easy it is to be mistaken. Just because I play the fool in front of strangers, tell them funny little stories, just because I'm so anxious to please, you've decided that I am a jolly fellow. If I didn't need them, these strangers, I mean, I wouldn't so much as look at them . . . All the same, wherever it's safe to do so, I make fun of these very people, you know . . . However, I don't deceive myself; I know that some of these gentry need me, can't take a step without me, are bored when I'm not there, and think they have the right to despise me. But I don't owe them a thing. Take Natalya Petrovna, for instance . . . do you think I don't see right through her? *Mimics Natalya Petrovna.* 'My dear doctor, I do love you so . . . you have such a wicked tongue . . .' ha-ha, go on cooing my little dove, coo . . . coo. Oh these ladies! They smile at you, make eyes at you – like that – but you can see it on their faces . . . they feel nothing but disgust for us . . . and what can you do? I understand all too well why she said horrid things about me today. Really, these fine ladies are extraordinary beings! Just because they wash in eau de Cologne every day, and don't mind what they say – and scatter their words carelessly, for you and me to pick up as best we can – because of that, these ladies imagine that one can't catch them by the tail. But that's not so at all. They are no different from the rest of us – sinful mortals like us all.

LIZAVETA BOGDANOVNA: Ignati Ilyich . . . you amaze me.

SHPIGELSKY: I knew I'd astonish you . . . Now you see that I'm not particularly jolly at all, and perhaps not too kind either . . . But I don't want to pretend to you that I am something I've never been. Whatever turns I may do in front of my betters, no one's ever seen me playing the part of the society fool – nobody has ever tweaked my nose. In fact, I'd say they're a little afraid of me; they know I can bite. Once, two or three years ago, a certain gentleman, one of those backwoodsmen, while we were all at table, suddenly stuck a radish in my hair, just for a bit of fun. What do you suppose I did? I didn't lose my temper, but quite coolly, in the politest possible manner, I called him out at once. The fellow almost had a stroke, he was so terrified. Our host made him apologise – the effect was marvellous! . . . I must admit I knew perfectly well that he wouldn't fight. But you must realise, Lizaveta Bogdanovna, that I am extremely vain. Well, there it is – that's how my life has turned out. I haven't much talent – I wasn't a good student. I'm not a good doctor; I won't hide that from you. If ever you fall ill when we're together, *I'm* not going to treat you. If I'd had the gifts or the education, I'd be in Petersburg, not here. But here, of course, they don't need a better doctor; I'm good enough for the locals. As for my actual character, I must warn you, Lizaveta Bogdanovna, that at home I'm liable to be rather gloomy, silent, exacting. If I am well served and have all my wishes attended to, I'm not against that; and I like people to take note of my habits, and provide me with good food. I'm not jealous, by the way, or mean, and when I'm not there you can do what you like. There is, of course, no question of anything like romantic love between us – you do realise that, I imagine. But I think that it's still possible to live under the same roof with me . . . provided everything is done the way I like it. And no tears while I'm about. I can't stand tears. And I don't nag or find fault all the time. There's my confession for you. Well, ma'am, what do you say to that?

LIZAVETA BOGDANOVNA: What can I say, Ignati Ilyich . . . if you haven't deliberately blackened yourself . . .

SHPIGELSKY: Blackened myself? In what way? Don't forget – anyone else in my place wouldn't have said a word about his faults – would've been only too pleased that you hadn't noticed anything – and then, once the wedding is over, no good – too late . . . But I'm too proud for that. *Lizaveta Bogdanovna glances at him.* Yes, yes, proud . . . in spite of your looking at me like that. I don't propose to pretend or to lie to my future wife, not for fifteen thousand, or a hundred thousand either. To a stranger I'd bow and scrape for a sack of flour – that's what I'm like. With strangers I can smile obsequiously, and at the same time be thinking 'What a fool you are, my boy, how easy it is to hook you.' But to you I'm saying what I think. That is, I won't say all I think, to be sure, even to you;

but at least I am not going to deceive you. I expect you think I'm eccentric – yes, of course, but you wait – one day I shall tell you the story of my life; you'll be astonished at how well I've lasted. You didn't eat off gold plate yourself, I imagine, but still, I'm pretty sure, my dear, that you've no idea what real hopeless poverty is like . . . However, I'll tell you about all that at some other time. And now . . . you'd better think over what I've just had the honour of telling you . . . Think about it carefully, this little matter, when you're alone, and let me have your decision. So far as I can tell, you're a sensible woman. You . . . By the way, how old are you?

LIZAVETA BOGDANOVNA: I . . . I'm . . . thirty.

SHPIGELSKY *calmly:* That's not true. You're at least forty.

LIZAVETA BOGDANOVNA *flaring up:* I'm *not* forty at all, I'm thirty-six.

SHPIGELSKY: All the same, not thirty. Now *that*, Lizaveta Bogdanovna, is the kind of thing you *must* stop doing . . . A married woman of thirty-six isn't old. And you should stop taking snuff. *Getting up.* I think it's stopped raining.

LIZAVETA BOGDANOVNA *also getting up:* Yes, it has.

SHPIGELSKY: So, if you could give me your answer one of these days?

LIZAVETA BOGDANOVNA: You shall have my decision tomorrow.

SHPIGELSKY: Now, that's what I like. That shows real sense! Splendid! Come along now, Lizaveta Bogdanovna, give me your arm, let's go back.

LIZAVETA BOGDANOVNA *giving him her arm:* Yes, let's.

SHPIGELSKY: Oh, by the way . . . I haven't kissed your hand . . . And yet, one is supposed to. Well, this once, here goes! *Kisses her hand. Lizaveta Bogdanovna blushes.* That's it. *Goes to the garden door.*

LIZAVETA BOGDANOVNA *stopping:* So you think, Ignati Ilyich, that Mikhailo Aleksandrych isn't really a dangerous man?

SHPIGELSKY: I shouldn't say so.

LIZAVETA BOGDANOVNA: Well, do you know, Ignati Ilyich, I think that Natalya Petrovna for some time now . . . I think that Mr Belyaev . . . She has been paying him a good deal of attention, don't you think? And what about Verochka? Isn't that the reason why today . . .

SHPIGELSKY *interrupting her:* I forgot to tell you one more thing, Lizaveta Bogdanovna. I'm tremendously inquisitive myself, but I can't bear inquisitive women – I mean – let me explain: in my book a wife must be both curious and observant (which can actually be very useful to her husband), but only provided that it's directed towards other people . . . do you follow me: only other people. However, if you must know my opinion about Natalya Petrovna, Vera Aleksandrovna, Mr Belyaev and everybody else here, then listen, and I shall sing you a little song. My voice is appalling, but you won't mind that.

LIZAVETA BOGDANOVNA *surprised:* A song!

SHPIGELSKY: Listen: First verse:

> Granny had a small grey goat
> Granny had a small grey goat
> That's it, that's it
> Grey kid – O!
> That's it! that's it!
> Grey kid – O.

> Second verse:
> Little kid – O! – went to play in the wood,
> Little kid – O! – went to play in the wood.
> That's it! that's it!
> In the wood to play
> That's it! that's it!
> In the wood to play!

LIZAVETA BOGDANOVNA: I am afraid I don't understand.

SHPIGELSKY: Well then, listen: third verse:

> The grey old wolves ate up the goat,
> The grey old wolves ate up the goat.

Skips up and down.

> That's it! that's it!
> Ate up the kid
> That's it! that's it!
> Ate up the kid.

Now, let's go. As a matter of fact, I must have a talk with Natalya Petrovna. Maybe she won't bite me. Unless I'm mistaken she still needs me. Come along. *Both go into the garden.*

KATYA *cautiously comes out from behind the pillar:* At last! I thought they'd never go! Oh, that wicked, nasty doctor man . . . talk, talk, talk.

God only knows what it's all about! And his singing! Aleksei Nikolaich may have gone back to the house during all that – that's what I'm afraid of . . . why did they need to come just here! *Goes up to the window.* And Lizaveta Bogdanovna? She'll be the doctoress, . . . *(Laughs)* that's what she'll be . . . Well, I don't envy her. *Looks out of the window.* The grass looks freshly washed . . . it smells so nice . . . it must be the wild cherry . . . Ah, here he comes. *After waiting a little.* Aleksei Nikolaich! . . . Aleksei Nikolaich!

BELYAEV *off-stage:* Who's calling me? Is it you, Katya? *Comes up to the window.* What do you want?

KATYA: Come in here please . . . I've something to tell you.

BELYAEV: Oh! very well. *Leaves the window and a moment later enters through the door.* Here I am.

KATYA: You didn't get wet?

BELYAEV: No, I've been sitting in the greenhouse with Potap . . . He's your uncle isn't he?

KATYA: Yes, sir, he's my uncle.

BELYAEV: How pretty you look today! *Katya smiles and lowers her eyes. Belyaev takes a peach from his pocket.* Would you like it?

KATYA *refusing it:* No, thank you very much – you eat it yourself.

BELYAEV: I didn't refuse, did I, when you offered me those raspberries yesterday? Take it . . . I picked it for you . . . I really did.

KATYA: Oh well, thank you very much. *Takes the peach.*

BELYAEV: That's better. Now then, what is it you wanted to tell me?

KATYA: The young lady . . . Vera Aleksandrovna asked me . . . she would like to see you.

BELYAEV: Oh, I'll go and see her at once.

KATYA: No, sir . . . she's coming here herself. She wants to have a talk with you.

BELYAEV *with some astonishment:* She wants to come here?

KATYA: Yes, sir, here. You see . . . nobody ever comes here – you won't be disturbed in here. *Sighs.* She loves you very much, Aleksei Nikolaich . . . she's so kind. I'll fetch her now, shall I? You'll wait?

BELYAEV: Yes, of course, of course.

KATYA: Just a moment . . . *Goes and then stops.* Aleksei Nikolaich, is it true what they say, that you're going away?

BELYAEV: That I'm? . . . No . . . who told you?

KATYA: So you won't be going? Oh, thank God for that! *With embarrassment.* We'll be here in a moment. *Goes through the door which leads into the house.*

BELYAEV *remaining motionless for some time:* What strange, extraordinary things are happening to me. I must say, I never expected all this. Vera loves me . . . Natalya Petrovna knows it . . . Vera herself told her everything . . . wonderful! Vera – such a kind, sweet child. But . . . what's the meaning of this note? *Extracts out of his pocket a scrap of paper.* It's from Natalya Petrovna . . . in pencil: 'Don't go away, don't decide anything until I've discussed it with you.' What does she want to talk to me about? *After a silence.* The most ridiculous thoughts are coming into my head! I must say, all this is terribly embarrassing. If somebody had told me, a month ago, that I . . . I . . . I simply can't get over that conversation with Natalya Petrovna. Why is my heart beating like this? And now Vera wants to see me . . . What shall I say to her! At least I'll find out what it is all about . . . *Looks at the note again.* It's all very strange, very strange. *The door opens very quietly; he quickly hides the note. Vera and Katya appear in the doorway. He goes up to them. Vera is very pale, doesn't raise her eyes and doesn't move.*

KATYA: Don't be afraid, miss, you go up to him; I'll be on the lookout . . . don't be afraid. *To Belyaev.* Oh, Aleksei Nikolaich! *She closes the windows, goes to the garden and locks the door behind her.*

BELYAEV: Vera Aleksandrovna . . . you wanted to see me. Why don't you come over here, do sit down here. *Takes her by the hand and leads her to the bench. Vera sits down.* There we are. *Looking at her with surprise.* You've been crying.

VERA *without lifting her eyes:* No, it's nothing . . . I came to ask you to forgive me, Aleksei Nikolaich.

BELYAEV: Forgive you for what?

VERA: I heard . . . you had a disagreeable talk with Natalya Petrovna . . . you're going away . . . you've been dismissed.

BELYAEV: Who told you that?

VERA: Natalya Petrovna herself . . . I met her after your talk with her . . . She told me that you yourself didn't want to stay here any longer. But I believe that she ordered you to go.

BELYAEV: Tell me, do they know about this in the house?

VERA: No . . . only Katya . . . I had to tell her . . . I wanted to speak to you and ask you to forgive me. You can imagine how badly I

feel about this . . . after all, I'm the cause of it all, Aleksei Nikolaich, it's all my fault.

BELYAEV: Yours, Vera Aleksandrovna?

VERA: How could I have expected . . . Natalya Petrovna . . .
however, I forgive her . . . and you must forgive her too . . . this
morning I was a silly child, but now . . . *She stops.*

BELYAEV: Nothing's been settled yet, Vera Aleksandrovna . . . I
may be staying.

VERA *sadly:* You say nothing's been settled, Aleksei Nikolaich . . .
no, everything has been settled, it's all finished. When I think of
how you are with me now, when only yesterday, do you remember, in the garden . . . *After a silence.* Yes, I can see that Natalya
Petrovna has told you everything.

BELYAEV *embarrassed:* Vera Aleksandrovna . . .

VERA: She told you everything, I can see that . . . She set a trap for
me, and like a fool I ran straight into it . . . But she gave herself
away too . . . I'm not such a child as all that. *Lowering her voice.* Oh
no!

BELYAEV: What do you mean?

VERA *glancing at him:* Aleksei Nikolaich, did you yourself really want
to leave us?

BELYAEV: Yes.

VERA: Why? *Belyaev is silent.* You don't answer me?

BELYAEV: Vera Aleksandrovna, you are *not* mistaken – Natalya
Petrovna did tell me everything.

VERA *in a faint voice:* What, for example?

BELYAEV: Vera Aleksandrovna . . . I really can't . . . Surely you
understand me . . .

VERA: Perhaps she told you that I love you?

BELYAEV *hesitantly:* Yes.

VERA *quickly:* But it's untrue . . .

BELYAEV *embarrassed:* What! . . .

VERA *covers her face with her hands and whispers expressionlessly through her
fingers:* No, I certainly didn't tell her that, I can't remember . . .
Lifting her head. Oh, how cruel she has been to me! And to you . . .
you're going away because of this?

BELYAEV: Vera Aleksandrovna, don't you think yourself . . .

VERA *glancing at him:* He doesn't love me. *Covers her face again.*

BELYAEV *sitting down next to her and taking her hands:* Vera

Aleksandrovna, give me your hand . . . Listen, there mustn't be any misunderstanding between us: I love you like a sister; I love you, because one cannot not love you . . . Forgive me if I . . . I've never been in such a situation in all my life . . . I wouldn't want to hurt you . . . I shan't pretend to you: I know that you like me, that you've grown fond of me . . . but do ask yourself, what could possibly come of it? I'm only twenty and I haven't a penny in the world. Please don't be angry with me. I really don't know what to say to you.

VERA *taking her hands from her face and looking at him:* As if I'd demanded anything from you. Oh God! But why so cruelly, so mercilessly . . . *She stops.*

BELYAEV: Vera Aleksandrovna, I didn't want to distress you.

VERA: I'm not accusing you, Aleksei Nikolaich – what fault is it of yours? It's my fault, entirely mine, and I've been punished for it. I don't accuse her either; I know she's a kind woman but she couldn't control herself . . . she lost her head.

BELYAEV *astonished:* Lost her head?

VERA *turning towards him:* Natalya Petrovna loves you, Belyaev.

BELYAEV: What?

VERA: She is in love with you.

BELYAEV: What *are* you saying?

VERA: I know what I'm saying. I've grown years older today . . . I'm not a child any longer, believe me. She decided to be jealous . . . of me. *With a bitter smile.* What do you say to that?

BELYAEV: But that's quite impossible.

VERA: Impossible, but . . . then why did she suddenly decide to marry me off to that gentleman, what *is* his name, Bolshintsov? Why did she get the doctor to come and see me? Why did she try and talk me into it herself? Oh, I know what I'm saying! If you could have seen, Belyaev, her entire face changed when I told her . . . Oh, you can't imagine the cunning, the tricks she used, to worm this confession out of me . . . Yes, she loves you; that's all too clear . . .

BELYAEV: Vera Aleksandrovna, you are mistaken, I assure you.

VERA: No, I am not. Believe me, I am not mistaken. If she doesn't love you, why has she tortured me like this? What have I done to her? *Bitterly.* Jealousy, that's the excuse for everything. Oh, why go on! . . . And now, why is she telling you to go? Because she thinks that you . . . you and I . . . Oh, she needn't feel the slightest anxiety! You can stay! *Covers her face with her hands.*

BELYAEV: So far she hasn't ordered me to go . . . I've already told you that nothing has been decided yet . . .

VERA *suddenly lifting her head and looking at him:* Really?

BELYAEV: Yes . . . but why are you looking at me like that?

VERA *as if to herself:* Ah, I understand . . . yes, yes . . . she must still be hoping . . . *The door to the corridor opens quickly and Natalya Petrovna appears in the doorway: she stops on seeing Vera and Belyaev.*

BELYAEV: What are you saying?

VERA: Yes, now it's all quite clear to me . . . She's come to her senses, she's realised that I am no danger to her! And actually, what am I? A silly little girl – whereas she!

BELYAEV: Vera Aleksandrovna, how can you think . . .

VERA: Anyway, who can tell? Maybe she's right . . . maybe you do love her.

BELYAEV: I?

VERA *rising:* Yes, you; why are you blushing?

BELYAEV: I, Vera Aleksandrovna?

VERA: Do you love her, could you love her? . . . you're not answering my question?

BELYAEV: Good God, what do you want me to answer? Vera Aleksandrovna, you're so agitated . . . do try and be calm, for goodness sake . . .

VERA *turning away from him:* You're treating me like a child . . . like someone who doesn't deserve a serious answer . . . you simply want to get rid of me . . . you're trying to comfort me. *Makes as if to leave, but at the sight of Natalya Petrovna suddenly stops.* Natalya Petrovna . . . *Belyaev quickly looks round.*

NATALYA PETROVNA *taking a few steps forward:* Yes, it's me. *She speaks with a certain effort.* I've come to fetch you, Verochka.

VERA *slowly and coldly:* What made you come to this particular place? You must have been looking for me.

NATALYA PETROVNA: Yes, I was looking for you. You aren't careful enough, Verochka . . . I've told you that more than once . . . and you, Aleksei Nikolaich, you've forgotten your promise . . . you've deceived me.

VERA: That's enough! Do stop, Natalya Petrovna. *Natalya Petrovna looks at her with amazement.* Don't go on talking to me as if I were a child . . . *Dropping her voice.* From today, I'm a woman . . . a woman like you.

NATALYA PETROVNA *taken aback:* Vera . . .

VERA *almost whispering:* He didn't deceive you . . . it wasn't he who asked to see me. He doesn't love me. You know that, you've no cause for jealousy.

NATALYA PETROVNA *with growing amazement:* Vera!

VERA: Believe me . . . there's no point in all your scheming, none of this will do you any good . . . I can see through it all now, I assure you. I'm not your ward, Natalya Petrovna, you needn't watch over me *(with irony)* like an older sister . . . *Moves towards her.* I'm your rival.

NATALYA PETROVNA: Vera, you are forgetting yourself . . .

VERA: Perhaps I am . . . But who has driven me to this? I don't understand myself how I've found the courage to speak to you like this . . . Perhaps I'm talking like this because I've nothing left to hope for, because you chose to stamp on me and crush me . . . And you succeeded . . . succeeded completely. But listen: I don't intend to try and make rings round you as you have done with me . . . you'd better know *(pointing to Belyaev)* that I've told him everything.

NATALYA PETROVNA: What could you tell him?

VERA: What? *With irony.* Why, everything that I happened to notice. You hoped to worm everything out of me without giving yourself away. You were wrong, Natalya Petrovna. You over-estimated your powers . . .

NATALYA PETROVNA: Vera, Vera, this is mad talk.

VERA *in a whisper, moving still closer to her:* Tell me that I've made a mistake . . . tell me that you don't love him . . . He told me, you know, that he doesn't love me . . . *Natalya Petrovna is embarrassed and silent; Vera stands without moving for a while and suddenly puts her hand to her forehead.* Natalya Petrovna, please forgive me . . . I . . . I don't know what's wrong with me . . . forgive me, don't hold it against me. *Bursts into floods of tears and quickly goes through the door into the corridor. Silence.*

BELYAEV *going towards Natalya Petrovna:* I can assure you, Natalya Petrovna . . .

NATALYA PETROVNA *looking fixedly at the floor, holds out her hand in his direction:* Stay, Aleksei Nikolaich. It is true: Vera is right . . . It's time . . . time I stopped cheating. I've behaved abominably towards her and towards you too. You have every right to despise me. *Belyaev makes an involuntary movement.* I've sunk low in my own eyes. There's only one way left for me to regain your respect: honesty, complete honesty, whatever the consequences. Moreover, I'm seeing you for the last time – this is the last time that I shall speak to you. I love you. *She continues not looking at him.*

BELYAEV: You, Natalya Petrovna! . . .

NATALYA PETROVNA: Yes, I. I love you. Vera did not deceive herself, and she didn't deceive you. I have loved you from the very first day you came here, but I've known it myself only since yesterday. I am not going to try to justify my conduct . . . it was unworthy of me . . . But at least now you can understand, and you can forgive me. Yes, I was jealous of Vera; yes, in my mind I had married her off to Bolshintsov to get her away from myself and from you; yes, I took advantage of my years, my position, to pry her secret out of her, and – I didn't expect that, of course – I gave myself away. I love you, Belyaev; but understand: it is only pride that forces me to admit this . . . The comedy I've been playing until now has finally revolted me. You can't stay here . . . Anyhow, after what I've just said to you, you'll probably feel very uncomfortable in my presence and you yourself will want to get away as soon as possible. I feel certain of that. And this certainty has given me courage. I admit I don't want you to think too badly of me. You know everything now . . . perhaps I've spoilt it all for you . . . perhaps if all this hadn't happened you might have fallen in love with Verochka . . . I've only got one excuse, Aleksei Nikolaich . . . it was all beyond my power. *She falls silent. She says all this in a rather quiet, even voice, not looking at Belyaev. He remains silent. She continues with some agitation, still not looking at him.* You don't answer me? . . . But I understand that. There's nothing you can say to me . . . The situation of a man who has just received a declaration of love, when he feels none himself, is very painful. I thank you for your silence. Believe me, when I told you . . . that I love you, it wasn't a move in a game . . . as before; it wasn't calculated; on the contrary: I wanted to throw off the mask which, I can assure you, I never got used to . . . And anyway, what is the point of carrying on with all this artificial talk, all this pretence, when all is known; why go on acting, when there's actually no one to deceive? Everything is over between us now. I don't wish to keep you. You can go without saying a word to me, without so much as saying goodbye to me. Not only shall I not think it discourteous, but on the contrary – I shall be grateful to you. There are occasions when delicacy is out of place – when it's worse than rudeness. Obviously we weren't destined to get to know each other. Goodbye. Yes, we weren't destined to get to know each other . . . But I hope that you will at least no longer think of me as the cunning, secretive, despotic creature you took me for . . . Goodbye, forever. *Belyaev wants to say something, but is too flustered to be able to speak.* You aren't going?

BELYAEV *bows, makes as if to go, but after a certain inner struggle comes back:* No, I cannot go away . . . *Natalya Petrovna looks at him for the first time.* I can't go away like this! . . . Listen, Natalya Petrovna, you've just told me . . . that you don't want me to go away with too un-favourable an impression of you, but neither do I want you to remember me as a man who . . . oh God, I don't know how to say it . . . Natalya Petrovna, forgive me . . . I don't know how to talk to ladies . . . up to now, I've known women . . . who weren't at all like this. You say that we are not destined to know each other, but good heavens, how could I – a simple, scarcely–educated boy – how could I even begin to think of a closer relationship with you? Have you thought about what you are and what I am! How could I dare imagine . . . with your education . . . but why speak of education . . . Look at me . . . this old coat and your scented dresses . . . Oh God – yes, it's true, I *was* afraid of you . . . And I'm still afraid of you now . . . I'm not exaggerating – I looked on you as being of a higher order – and now . . . you, you tell me that you love me . . . you, Natalya Petrovna! Me! . . . I feel my heart is beating as it has never done before in my life; it is not just amazement that makes it beat, not vanity, not because I'm flattered . . . oh no, no! It's nothing to do with vanity. But I cannot . . . I cannot go away like this, whatever you may say.

NATALYA PETROVNA *after a pause, as if talking to herself:* What have I done?

BELYAEV: Natalya Petrovna, for God's sake, believe me . . .

NATALYA PETROVNA *in a changed voice:* Aleksei Nikolaich, if I didn't know you to be an honourable man, a man incapable of lying, God only knows what I might think. I might have regretted that I had been so frank with you. But I do believe you. I don't want to hide my feelings from you: I'm grateful to you for what you have just said. I know now why we didn't become friends . . . So it wasn't anything in *me* that repelled you . . . it's only my position . . . *Stops.* It's all for the best, of course . . . but now it'll be easier for me to part with you . . . Goodbye. *Makes as if to go.*

BELYAEV *after a silence:* Natalya Petrovna, I know that it's impossible for me to stay here . . . But I cannot convey to you what is going on inside me. You love me . . . I cannot even utter these words without a sense of terror . . . all this is so new to me . . . It seems to me that I am seeing you and hearing you for the first time, but I am sure of one thing: I must go . . . I feel that I couldn't be answerable for anything . . .

NATALYA PETROVNA *in a weak voice:* Yes, Belyaev, you must go . . . Now, since you have explained yourself, you can go away . . . And is it really possible, in spite of everything I did . . . Oh, believe me, if I'd had the remotest suspicion of what you have now told me – this confession, Belyaev, would have died in me . . . I only wanted to clear up all the misunderstandings, I wanted to make a full confession, to punish myself, I wanted to end it, to cut the last thread. If I could only have conceived . . . *Covers her face with her hands.*

BELYAEV: I believe you, Natalya Petrovna, I believe you. Why, I myself, only a quarter of an hour ago . . . how could I have imagined . . . It was only today, during our last meeting before dinner, that for the first time I felt something extraordinary, something I'd never experienced before, as though a hand was clutching at my heart, and a feeling of warmth began to fill my breast . . . It's true that before I seemed to avoid you somehow, it was almost as if I didn't like you; but when you told me today that Vera Aleksandrovna thought . . . *Stops.*

NATALYA PETROVNA *with an involuntary smile of happiness on her lips:* No, no, you mustn't go on, Belyaev; we mustn't think these thoughts. We mustn't forget that we are talking to each other for the last time . . . That you are leaving tomorrow . . .

BELYAEV: Oh, yes! Tomorrow I'll be gone! I could go now . . . It will all pass . . . I don't want to exaggerate, you see . . . I'll go away . . . and after that, what will be, will be! But there's one thing I shall never forget – I shall remember forever that you loved me . . .

How could it be that I did not know you until now? You are looking at me now . . . how is it possible that I could ever have tried to avoid your eyes . . . could ever have felt shy in your presence?

NATALYA PETROVNA *with a smile:* You told me just now that you were afraid of me.

BELYAEV: Did I? *After a silence.* That's true . . . I'm astonished at myself . . . I, is it I who is talking to you so boldly? I don't recognise myself.

NATALYA PETROVNA: And you are not deceiving yourself?

BELYAEV: In what way?

NATALYA PETROVNA: In believing that your feeling towards me . . . *Shudders.* God, what am I doing . . . Listen, Belyaev . . . please help me . . . no woman was ever in such a situation. I haven't the strength, I tell you. Perhaps it is all for the best, finished and done with at one stroke. But at least we've come to know each other . . . give me your hand – and goodbye for . . . ever . . .

BELYAEV *takes her hand:* Natalya Petrovna . . . I don't know what to say before we part . . . my heart is so full . . . May God give you . . . *He stops and presses her hand to his lips.* Goodbye. *Makes as if to go into the garden.*

NATALYA PETROVNA *following him with a glance:* Belyaev . . .

BELYAEV *turning round:* Natalya Petrovna?

NATALYA PETROVNA *after a short silence, in a weak voice:* Stay . . .

BELYAEV: What?

NATALYA PETROVNA: Stay, and let God be our judge. *She hides her face in her hands.*

BELYAEV *goes up to her quickly and holds out his hands towards her:* Natalya Petrovna . . . *At this moment the door from the garden opens and Rakitin appears in the doorway. He looks at them for some time and suddenly goes up to them.*

RAKITIN *loudly:* They are looking for you everywhere, Natalya Petrovna. *Natalya Petrovna and Belyaev look round.*

NATALYA PETROVNA *taking her hands from her face, and, like someone coming to:* Oh, it's you . . . Who is looking for me? *Belyaev, flustered, bows to Natalya Petrovna and wants to leave.* You are going, Aleksei Nikolaich . . . Well . . . don't forget, you do know . . . *He bows again and goes into the garden.*

RAKITIN: Arkadi is looking for you . . . I must say, I didn't expect to find you here . . . But I happened to be passing . . .

NATALYA PETROVNA *with a smile:* You heard our voices . . . I met Aleksei Nikolaich here . . . and we had a brief mutual explanation, he and I . . . Today seems to be a day of explanations, but now we can go back into the house . . . *Makes to go to the door leading to the corridor.*

RAKITIN *somewhat agitated:* May I be told . . . what decision . . .

NATALYA PETROVNA *pretending to be surprised:* What decision? . . . I don't understand you.

RAKITIN *after a long silence, sadly:* In that case, I understand everything.

NATALYA PETROVNA: Well, there it is . . . Again these mysterious references! Yes, I had a talk with him, and now everything is in order . . . It was all nonsense, all exaggerated . . . Everything that you and I talked about, it was all childish nonsense. We must forget it.

RAKITIN: I'm not putting questions to you, Natalya Petrovna.

NATALYA PETROVNA *in an artificially casual manner:* Oh dear, what was it I wanted to say to you . . . I don't remember. It doesn't matter. Let's go. It's all over, all that . . . it's finished.

RAKITIN *looking at her intently:* Yes, it's all over. How annoyed you must feel with yourself now . . . for talking so openly today . . . *He turns away.*

NATALYA PETROVNA: Rakitin . . . *He glances at her again: she evidently does not know what to say.* You haven't spoken to Arkadi yet?

RAKITIN: No, ma'am, I have not — I haven't had time to prepare myself . . . You realise that I shall have to make up a story . . .

NATALYA PETROVNA: Really, this is quite intolerable! What do they all want from me? They watch every step I make. Rakitin, I really do feel ashamed before you.

RAKITIN: Oh, Natalya Petrovna, there's no need to worry yourself . . . Why should you? It's all in the normal course of things . . . But it's clear that Mr Belyaev is rather a novice in these matters! Why was he so embarrassed? Why did he run away? . . . However, in time . . . *(speaking* sotto voce, *rapidly)* you'll both learn how to act your parts. *Loudly.* Let's go. *Natalya Petrovna wants to go up to him, but stops. At this moment, behind the garden door, Islayev's voice is heard:* 'He went this way did you say?' — *after which, enter Islayev and Shpigelsky.*

ISLAYEV: Here we are . . . he *is* here! Ho, ho, ho! And Natalya Petrovna is here too. *Goes up to her.* What's this? Continuation of this morning's conference? It must be an important matter.

RAKITIN: I met Natalya Petrovna here . . .

ISLAYEV: Met? *Looks round him.* It's not exactly an obvious meeting place, is it?

NATALYA PETROVNA: Well, *you* made your way here, after all . . .

ISLAYEV: I came here because . . . *Stops.*

NATALYA PETROVNA: You were looking for me?

ISLAYEV *after a silence:* Yes — I was looking for you. Come back to the house, won't you? Tea is ready. It'll soon be dark.

NATALYA PETROVNA *takes his arm:* Let's go.

ISLAYEV *looking round:* This place could be turned into two quite good rooms for the gardeners — or another servants' hall. What do you think, Shpigelsky?

SHPIGELSKY: Yes, it certainly could.

ISLAYEV: Let's go by the garden, Natasha. *Goes to the garden door. During this entire scene he does not once look at Rakitin. In the doorway, he half turns.* What are you waiting, for, gentlemen? Come and have tea. *Leaves with Natalya Petrovna.*

SHPIGELSKY: Well, Mikhailo Aleksandrych, let's go . . . your arm . . . evidently we are meant to bring up the rear.

RAKITIN *furiously* May I inform you, Doctor, that I am sick and tired of you.

SHPIGELSKY *with affected amiability:* Oh, Mikhailo Aleksandrych, if only you knew how tired I am of myself! *Rakitin can't help smiling.* Let's go, let's go . . . *Both go through the garden door.*

END OF ACT FOUR

ACT FIVE

The scene is the same as in Acts One and Three. Morning. Islayev is sitting at the table and is looking through some papers. He suddenly gets up.

ISLAYEV: No! It is no good – I can't work today. It's as if a nail has been driven into my head. *Walks up and down.* I must say, I didn't expect this; I didn't expect to be upset like this. What am I to do, that's the problem. *Thinks for a while and then shouts.* Matvei!

MATVEI *entering:* Yes, sir?

ISLAYEV: Call the bailiff . . . tell the men digging at the weir to wait for me . . . Off you go, then.

MATVEI: Yes, sir. *Exits.*

ISLAYEV *turns to the table and riffles through the papers:* Yes . . . that's the problem!

ANNA SEMYONOVNA *entering, and going up to Islayev:* Arkasha . . .

ISLAYEV: Ah, it's you, Mama. How are you feeling?

ANNA SEMYONOVNA *sitting down on the sofa:* I'm quite well, thank God. *Sighs.* I'm well *(sighs still more audibly)*, thank God. *Seeing that Islayev is not listening to her, sighs very heavily and gives a slight moan.*

ISLAYEV: You're sighing – what's the matter?

ANNA SEMYONOVNA *sighs again, but not so heavily:* Oh, Arkasha, as if you didn't know what I'm sighing about.

ISLAYEV: What do you mean?

ANNA SEMYONOVNA *after a silence:* I'm your mother, Arkasha. Of course, you are a grown man, and a sensible one: but all the same, I *am* your mother. Mother – that is a great word.

ISLAYEV: Do explain yourself, please.

ANNA SEMYONOVNA: You know what I'm alluding to, my dear – your wife, Natasha . . . of course, she's an admirable woman and her behaviour until now has been exemplary . . . But she's still so young, Arkasha! And if one is young . . .

ISLAYEV: I see what you mean . . . you think that her relationship with Rakitin . . .

ANNA SEMYONOVNA: Good gracious no! I was not thinking . . .

ISLAYEV: You didn't let me finish . . . You think that her relationship with Rakitin is not altogether clear . . . These mysterious conversations, these tears – you think all that a little strange.

ANNA SEMYONOVNA: Tell me, Arkasha, did he tell you in the end what all those conversations were about? . . . He never told me anything.

ISLAYEV: I didn't try to find out, Mama, and he is evidently in no great hurry to satisfy my curiosity.

ANNA SEMYONOVNA: And what do you intend to do now?

ISLAYEV: Do, Mama? Why, nothing.

ANNA SEMYONOVNA: What do you mean, nothing?

ISLAYEV: I mean exactly that – nothing.

ANNA SEMYONOVNA *rising:* I must say, I am surprised. Of course, you are master in your own house, you know better than I do what is right and what is wrong. Still, have you thought about the consequences? . . .

ISLAYEV: Mama, I do assure you – there is nothing for you to worry about.

ANNA SEMYONOVNA: After all, my dear – I am a *mother* . . . However, you know best. *After a silence.* I confess I came here to ask if I could do anything to arrange matters between you . . .

ISLAYEV *sharply:* No, I really must ask you, Mama, not to worry about all this . . . Do me a favour!

ANNA SEMYONOVNA: As you wish, Arkasha, just as you wish. I won't say another word. I warned you, I've done my duty – and from now on, not another word will you hear from me.

ISLAYEV *after a short silence:* Are you going for a drive anywhere today?

ANNA SEMYONOVNA: But I really must warn you: you're too trusting, my dear boy, you judge everybody by yourself! Believe me: real friends are very rare these days!

ISLAYEV *impatiently:* Mama . . .

ANNA SEMYONOVNA: Very well – not a word, not another word. What's the use of my talking, an old woman like me, almost out of her mind! But I was brought up on different principles – and I did my best to instil them in you . . . Well, well, get on with your work, I shan't disturb you . . . I'm going. *Goes to the door and stops.* Well then? . . . Oh, well, you know best, you know best! *Exits.*

ISLAYEV *looking after her:* I wonder what it is that makes people who really do love you put all their fingers, one by one, into your wound? And yet they're convinced – that's what's so funny – that they're doing you good! However, I don't blame Mother: she means it all so well – how can you expect her not to try and give advice? But that's not the point . . . *Sitting down.* What am I to do? *After some thought, gets up.* Well, the simpler the better! Diplomatic subtleties are not for me . . . I'd be the first to get hopelessly entangled in them. *Rings. Matvei enters.* Is Mikhailo Aleksandrych in the house – do you know?

MATVEI: He is, sir. I've just seen his honour in the billiard-room.

ISLAYEV: Well, ask him to come and see me, will you?

MATVEI: Yes, sir. *Leaves.*

ISLAYEV *walks up and down:* I'm not used to imbroglios of this sort . . . I hope this sort of thing won't often happen . . . I've quite a strong constitution – but this isn't the kind of thing I can stand. *Puts a hand on his chest.* Phew! . . .

RAKITIN *embarrassed, comes in from the hall:* You wanted to see me?

ISLAYEV: Yes. *After a silence.* Michel, you owe me something, you know.

RAKITIN: Do I?

ISLAYEV: Yes, of course – have you forgotten your promise? About . . . Natasha's tears . . . and things generally . . . Do you remember when Mother and I came upon you, you told me that there was a secret between you, which you wanted to explain?

RAKITIN: Did I say a secret?

ISLAYEV: You did.

RAKITIN: What secret could there possibly be between us? We simply had a talk.

ISLAYEV: What was it about? And why was she crying?

RAKITIN: You know, Arkadi . . . There are some moments in a woman's life . . . even the happiest . . .

ISLAYEV: Rakitin, stop it, we can't go on like this. I can't bear to see you in this state . . . Your embarrassment distresses me more than it does you. *Takes him by the arm.* After all, we're old friends – you've known me since we were children. I am no good at being devious, and you've always been perfectly open with me. Let me ask you one thing . . . and I give you my word of honour that I shan't doubt the sincerity of your answer. You love my wife, don't you? *Rakitin glances at Islayev.* You understand me, is your love for her . . . I mean, what I want to say is – do you love my wife with the kind of love that it is . . . difficult to admit to a husband?

RAKITIN *after a silence, in a muffled voice:* Yes — I love your wife . . . in that way.

ISLAYEV *also after a silence:* Michel, thank you for being so frank. You are an honourable man. But what do we do now? Sit down, we must talk about this, you and I. *Rakitin sits down, Islayev walks up and down the room.* I know Natasha. I know what she is worth . . . but I know my own value too. Michel, you are a better man than I . . . don't interrupt me, please . . . I'm not as good as you. You are more intelligent, you're nicer, you've more charm than I. I'm a simple man. Natasha loves me — I think — but she has eyes . . . in short, she must find you attractive. There's something else I want to say: I noticed your feeling for each other a long time ago . . . I was always entirely sure of you both — so long as nothing came to the surface . . . oh, I don't know how to say these things! *Stops.* But after that scene yesterday, after your second meeting in the evening — what are we to do? If only I had been alone when I saw you — but there were witnesses: Mama, that rogue Shpigelsky . . . Well, Michel, what do you say, eh?

RAKITIN: You are absolutely right, Arkadi . . .

ISLAYEV: But that's not the point . . . the question is — what are we going to do? I must tell you, Michel, that although I'm a simple fellow — I know this much, that one mustn't ruin other people's lives — and that there are occasions when it's a sin to insist upon one's rights. It isn't something I've read in a book — it's my conscience that tells me. One must allow people their freedom . . . what? I mean — give them freedom! But this needs thinking over. It's too important.

RAKITIN *rising:* As a matter of fact, I've thought the whole thing over.

ISLAYEV: Well, and . . .?

RAKITIN: I must go . . . I am going away.

ISLAYEV *after a silence:* You think so? Go away completely?

RAKITIN: Yes.

ISLAYEV *again begins walking up and down the room:* That's . . . that's a very serious thing you've said! But perhaps you are right. It'll be very sad without you . . . And, God knows, it may not do much good . . . But you are **able** to see more clearly, you know better. I think you are right — **yes**, you are a danger to me. *With a sad smile.* Yes, you are dangerous. Now — about what I said a moment ago

. . . about freedom, I mean . . . and yet, it's possible I might not be able to survive it! To live without Natasha . . . *Waving his hand about.* And there's another thing I want to tell you: for some time now, especially in the last few days, I've noticed a great change in her. She seems to be in a state of perpetual agitation of some sort, and that frightens me. That's so, isn't it? I'm not mistaken, am I?

RAKITIN *bitterly:* Oh, no, you are not mistaken!

ISLAYEV: You see! . . . So you are going?

RAKITIN: Yes.

ISLAYEV: Hmm. It's all so sudden, a bolt from the blue. And did you have to look so embarrassed when Mother and I came upon you?

MATVEI *entering:* The bailiff is here, sir.

ISLAYEV: Let him wait! *Matvei exits.* Michel, you're not going away for long, are you? It's all utter nonsense, you know.

RAKITIN: I really don't know . . . I should think . . . for a long time.

ISLAYEV: You are not taking me for some kind of Othello, are you? I swear there's not been such a conversation between two friends since the world began! I can't part from you like this . . .

RAKITIN *shaking him by the hand:* You'll let me know when I may return.

ISLAYEV: There's absolutely nobody who can take your place! For goodness sake, not Bolshintsov!

RAKITIN: There are other people here . . .

ISLAYEV: Who? Krinitsyn, that silly fop? Belyaev, of course, is a dear, good fellow . . . but he's nothing compared to you – you're as far above him as the stars in the sky.

RAKITIN *acidly:* You think so? You don't know him, Arkadi . . . I should take a closer look at him if I were you . . . I really do advise you to do that . . . do you hear? He's a very . . . very remarkable man.

ISLAYEV: Bah! That's why you and Natasha said you were going to look after his education! *Glancing at the door.* Ah, here he is – coming this way, I think . . . *Rapidly.* So, my dear friend, that's settled – you're going away . . . for a short time . . . one of these days . . . There's no need to hurry – we must prepare Natasha . . . I'll reassure my mother . . . and God give you happiness! You've lifted a stone from my heart . . . Embrace me, my dearest friend.

Embraces him quickly, then turns towards Belyaev as he comes in. Ah . . . it's you! Well . . . well, how are you?

BELYAEV: Quite well, Arkadi Sergeich.

ISLAYEV: And where's Kolya?

BELYAEV: He's with Mr Schaaf.

ISLAYEV: Ah, very good. *Takes up his hat.* Well, gentlemen, I'm off, goodbye. I haven't been anywhere yet today – not to the weir, the building site . . . haven't even looked through my papers. *Rolls papers up and puts them under his arm.* Goodbye! Matvei! Matvei! come with me! *Exits.*

BELYAEV *going up to Rakitin:* How are you feeling today, Mikhailo Aleksandrych?

RAKITIN: Thank you, very much as usual – and how are you?

BELYAEV: I'm quite well.

RAKITIN: One can see that.

BELYAEV: Oh, why?

RAKITIN: Oh, one just can . . . by your face . . . Oh, you've put on a new coat today . . . And what do I see! A flower in your button-hole. *Belyaev blushes and pulls it out.* Oh why . . . why, you shouldn't . . . It's very nice. *After a silence.* By the way, Aleksei Nikolaich, if you need anything . . . I am going to town tomorrow.

BELYAEV: Tomorrow?

RAKITIN: Yes . . . and from there I may go to Moscow.

BELYAEV *surprised:* Moscow? But you told me only yesterday that you proposed to stay here for a month or so.

RAKITIN: Yes . . . but business . . . these things happen.

BELYAEV: And are you going away for long?

RAKITIN: I don't know . . . possibly for quite a long time.

BELYAEV: Do you mind my asking – does Natalya Petrovna know of your intention?

RAKITIN: No. Why do you ask me about her in particular?

BELYAEV: Do I? *Slightly flustered.* Oh, I don't know . . .

RAKITIN *after a silence, and after looking round:* Aleksei Nikolaich, as far as I can see we're alone in the room: isn't it rather odd that we should go on playing this charade with each other? Don't you think so?

BELYAEV: I don't understand you, Mikhailo Aleksandrych.

RAKITIN: Really? You really don't understand why I am going away?

BELYAEV: No.

RAKITIN: That's odd . . . however, I am prepared to believe you. Perhaps you really don't know the reason . . . Would you like me to tell you why I'm going away?

BELYAEV: If you would be so kind . . .

RAKITIN: You see, Aleksei Nikolaich – and by the way, I am relying upon your discretion – you found me just now with Arkadi Sergeich . . . we've been having a rather important conversation. As a result of that conversation, I've decided to leave. And do you know why? I am telling you all this because I regard you as an honourable man . . . He's conceived the idea that I . . . well, that I am in love with Natalya Petrovna. What do you think of that? Eh? It's a very strange idea – don't you think? But I am grateful to him, he didn't try to be cunning, didn't start following us, and so on, but talked to me simply and openly. And now – tell me – what would you have done in my place? Of course, his suspicions have absolutely no foundation, but he's worried . . . for the sake of a friend's peace of mind, decent men must sometimes be ready to sacrifice . . . their pleasures. That's why I am going away . . . I'm sure you will approve of my decision, won't you? And if you were in my position you would do just the same. You'd go away too, wouldn't you?

BELYAEV *after a silence:* Perhaps.

RAKITIN: I'm very glad to hear it . . . Of course, I don't deny that my decision to go has its comical side; it's as if I regarded myself as a dangerous man; but you see, Aleksei Nikolaich, a woman's honour is such an important thing . . . and besides – of course, I'm not saying this about Natalya Petrovna – but I have known women, innocent and pure in heart, who for all their intelligence are simply children, and who, precisely because of this purity and innocence, are more liable than others to be carried away by a sudden infatuation . . . and therefore – who can tell? – excessive caution is not such a bad thing in these cases – all the more because . . . By the way, Aleksei Nikolaich, perhaps you still imagine that love is the greatest bliss on earth?

BELYAEV *coldly:* I have, as yet, had no experience of it, but I think that to be loved by a woman whom one loves must be a great happiness.

RAKITIN: Long may you live under that pleasant illusion! I believe,

Aleksei Nikolaich, that every kind of love, whether happy or unhappy, is a real calamity if you surrender to it wholly . . . Wait! You may yet come to know how those gentle little hands can torture, with what solicitous tenderness they can rend the heart into little pieces . . . Just wait – you'll discover how much burning hatred is hidden within the most ardent love! You will think of me when you long for peace as a sick man longs for health, the most meaningless, commonplace kind of peace – when you will envy any man who is light-hearted and free . . . You wait! You'll find out what it means to be tied to a petticoat, to be a woman's slave, to feel the poison in one's veins – and how humiliating, how agonising such slavery is! . . . and finally, you'll learn what miserable trifles are bought at such high cost . . . But why am I saying all this to you? You won't believe me now. The point is that I am very glad that you approve . . . yes, yes . . . in situations of this kind one has to be careful.

BELYAEV *who all this time hasn't taken his eyes off Rakitin:* Thanks for the lecture, Mikhailo Aleksandrych, although I didn't need it.

RAKITIN *takes him by the arm:* Please forgive me – I didn't intend . . . it's not for me to lecture anybody . . . I was simply running on.

BELYAEV *with slight irony:* For no particular reason?

RAKITIN *slightly confused:* Precisely – for no particular reason. I only wanted . . . Aleksei Nikolaich, you haven't had the opportunity yet to study women closely. Women – are very capricious creatures.

BELYAEV: Why, whom are you talking about?

RAKITIN: Oh, nobody in particular.

BELYAEV: About women in general, then, is that it?

RAKITIN *with a forced smile:* Yes, perhaps. Well, I really don't know what made me adopt this schoolmasterly tone, but since we're saying goodbye, let me give you one piece of good advice. *Stops, and gives an impatient wave of the hand.* Oh, but really, it's hardly for me to offer advice! Please forgive me for all this idle chatter.

BELYAEV: Oh, not at all, not at all!

RAKITIN: Well then – you don't need anything in town?

BELYAEV: No, thank you. But I'm sorry that you're going.

RAKITIN: That's most kind of you . . . Believe me, I too . . . *From the door of the study come Natalya Petrovna and Vera. Vera looks very sad and pale.* I was very glad to make your acquaintance . . . *Shakes him by the hand again.*

NATALYA PETROVNA *looks at both of them for a while, then goes up to them:* Good day, gentlemen.

RAKITIN *turning quickly:* Good day, Natalya Petrovna, good day, Vera Aleksandrovna. *Belyaev silently bows to Natalya Petrovna and Vera. He looks flustered.*

NATALYA PETROVNA *to Rakitin:* And what have you been doing with yourself?

RAKITIN: Oh, nothing . . .

NATALYA PETROVNA: Well, Vera and I – we've already been out in the garden . . . it's so wonderful to be out on such a day . . . the lime trees smell so sweet, we spent the whole time just walking under them . . . so delightful to listen to the bees humming high above us in the shade . . . *Shyly, to Belyaev.* We had hoped to meet you there. *Belyaev is silent.*

RAKITIN *to Natalya Petrovna:* Ah! So you too have been gazing at the beauties of nature today . . . *After a silence.* Aleksei Nikolaich wasn't able to come into the garden . . . because he's put on his new coat . . .

BELYAEV *flaring up a little:* Yes, of course, it's the only one I possess, and it might easily get torn in the garden . . . Isn't that what you meant?

RAKITIN *flushing:* No, no, I didn't mean that at all . . .

Vera goes silently to the sofa on the right, sits down and picks up her work. Natalya Petrovna looks at Belyaev with a forced smile. A short but somewhat oppressive silence. Rakitin continues in a casual tone of voice, with some malice.

Oh, yes, and I forgot to tell you, Natalya Petrovna, I'm going away today . . .

NATALYA PETROVNA *with some agitation:* Going? Where?

RAKITIN: To the town . . . on business.

NATALYA PETROVNA: Not for long, I hope?

RAKITIN: That depends on how things go.

NATALYA PETROVNA: Mind you come back as soon as you can. *To Belyaev, without looking at him.* Aleksei Nikolaich, was it your drawings that Kolya was showing me – did you do them?

BELYAEV: Yes, ma'am . . . I . . . they're nothing much.

NATALYA PETROVNA: On the contrary, they're very charming. You have talent.

RAKITIN: I see you discover new qualities in Mr Belyaev every day.

NATALYA PETROVNA *coldly:* Possibly . . . so much the better for him. *To Belyaev.* You have other drawings, I expect – you must show them to me. *Belyaev bows.*

RAKITIN *who all this time has been nervously shifting from foot to foot:* Well, I think it's time I went and packed – goodbye. *Goes to the door of the hall.*

NATALYA PETROVNA *to him, as he is going:* But you'll be coming to say goodbye to us?

RAKITIN: Yes, of course.

BELYAEV *after some hesitation:* Mikhailo Aleksandrych, wait, I'll come with you. I must say a word to you.

RAKITIN: Oh? *They both go into the hall.*

NATALYA PETROVNA *remains standing in the middle of the stage; after a moment she sits down to the left. After remaining silent for a while:* Vera!

VERA *without lifting her head:* What do you want?

NATALYA PETROVNA: Vera, for heaven's sake, don't be like that with me . . . for goodness sake, Vera . . . Verochka. *Vera says nothing. Natalya Petrovna gets up, walks across the stage and quietly kneels before her. Vera wants to raise her, but turns away and covers her face.* Vera, forgive me; don't cry, Vera. I've behaved wickedly to you, I really am guilty. Can't you – can't you forgive me?

VERA *through her tears:* Get up, get up . . .

NATALYA PETROVNA: I shall not get up, Vera, until you forgive me. You're unhappy, I know . . . But do you think it's easier for me . . . Think . . . Vera . . . after all, you know everything . . . the only difference between us is that you have never done me any harm, whereas I . . .

VERA *bitterly:* The only difference! No, Natalya Petrovna, there's another kind of difference between us . . . Today, you're so gentle, so kind, so sweet –

NATALYA PETROVNA *interrupting her:* It's because I feel I'm guilty.

VERA: Really? Only because of that?

NATALYA PETROVNA *gets up and sits down beside her:* But what other reason could there be?

VERA: Natalya Petrovna, don't torture me any more, don't question me.

NATALYA PETROVNA *with a sigh:* Vera, I see that you can't forgive me.

VERA: You are so kind and gentle today because you feel that you are loved.

NATALYA PETROVNA *embarrassed:* Vera!

VERA *turning to her:* Well, isn't that the truth?

NATALYA PETROVNA *sadly:* Believe me, we are both equally unhappy.

VERA: He loves you!

NATALYA PETROVNA: Vera, why must we go on torturing each other? It's time we both came to our senses. Think of the position I'm in, the position we're both in. Remember that our secret — it's my fault of course — is known to two people here . . . *Stops.* Vera, rather than tormenting each other with suspicions and reproaches, wouldn't it be better for us both to think of how we can get out of this painful situation . . . how we can save ourselves . . . or do you think that I can stand all this agitation and anguish? Or have you forgotten who I am? But you're not listening to me.

VERA *looking at the floor pensively:* He loves you . . .

NATALYA PETROVNA: Vera, he is going away.

VERA *turning round:* Oh, do leave me alone . . .

Natalya Petrovna looks at her irresolutely. At this moment Islayev's voice is heard from the study: 'Natasha, hey, Natasha, where are you?'

NATALYA PETROVNA *getting up quickly and going to the door of the study:* I'm here . . . What is it?

ISLAYEV *off-stage:* Oh, do come here, I've something to tell you.

NATALYA PETROVNA: One minute. *She goes back to Vera and holds out her hand. Vera does not move. Natalya Petrovna sighs and goes to the study.*

VERA *alone, after a silence:* He loves her! . . . And I have to stay in her house . . . Oh, it's too much . . . *She hides her face in her hands and remains motionless. Shpigelsky's head appears round the door leading to the hall; he looks round cautiously and tiptoes towards Vera, who does not notice him.*

SHPIGELSKY *after standing in front of her for a while, with arms crossed and a nasty little smile:* Vera Aleksandrovna! . . . Vera Aleksandrovna . . .

VERA *lifting her head:* Who is it? Oh, it's you, Doctor.

SHPIGELSKY: What's the matter, young lady, are you unwell? Is that it?

VERA: No, it's nothing.

SHPIGELSKY: Let me feel your pulse. *Feels pulse.* Hmm, why is it so fast? My dear, dear young lady . . . you won't listen to me. But I'm doing it all for your good, you know.

VERA *with a look of resolution:* Ignati Ilyich . . .

SHPIGELSKY *with a quick, sharp look:* Yes, Vera Aleksandrovna . . . Goodness, what a look – I'm listening to you.

VERA: That gentleman . . . Bolshintsov, your friend – is he really a good man?

SHPIGELSKY: My friend Bolshintsov? The most excellent, most honourable man . . . he's virtue incarnate.

VERA: He's not unkind, then?

SHPIGELSKY: Oh, no, he's the soul of kindness, he's not a man, he's a lump of dough, you can simply take him and mould him. Why, you won't find anyone so utterly kind in the whole wide world, not if you searched with a candle by daylight. He's not a man, he's a gentle dove.

VERA: You vouch for him?

SHPIGELSKY *puts one hand on his heart, raises the other:* As I would for myself.

VERA: In that case, you can tell him . . . that I'm willing to marry him.

SHPIGELSKY *amazed and overjoyed:* No, really?

VERA: Only as soon as possible – do you hear? It must be as soon as possible.

SHPIGELSKY: Tomorrow, if you like . . . That's absolutely marvellous, Vera Aleksandrovna! What a wonderful young woman you are! I shall dash over and tell him. Oh, he'll be so delighted . . . what an unexpected turn – I know he worships, absolutely worships you, Vera Aleksandrovna.

VERA *impatiently:* I didn't ask you that, Ignati Ilyich.

SHPIGELSKY: Anything you say, Vera Aleksandrovna, anything you say. Oh! but you will be happy with him, you'll be grateful to me, you'll see . . . *Vera again makes an impatient gesture.* Very well, not a word, not a word! So I can tell him, then . . .

VERA: You can, you can.

SHPIGELSKY: Very good, then, off I go. At once. Goodbye. *Listens.* By the way, someone's coming. *Goes to the study concealing a look of astonishment.* Goodbye. *Goes.*

VERA *following him with a look:* Anything on earth rather than stay here . . . *Gets up.* Yes; I've made up my mind, I'm not going to stay in this house . . . not for anything in the world. I can't bear that meek expression, that smile – I can't bear to see her so . . . at peace and basking in her happiness. She *is* happy, however sad and gloomy she may pretend to be . . . Her caresses are unbearable. *Belyaev appears in the door to the hall; looks round him, and goes up to Vera.*

BELYAEV *in a low voice:* Vera Aleksandrovna, are you alone?

VERA *looks round, shudders, and after a short silence manages to utter:* Yes.

BELYAEV: I'm glad you are alone . . . otherwise I wouldn't have come. Vera Aleksandrovna, I came to say goodbye to you.

VERA: Are you going away too?

BELYAEV: Yes . . . I too. *With deep agitation.* You see, Vera Aleksandrovna, I can't stay here. My being here has caused too much harm as it is. Besides, I've somehow – I really don't know how – I've managed to disturb your peace of mind, and Natalya Petrovna's, and upset relations between old friends. It's entirely thanks to me that Mr Rakitin is leaving the house, that you've quarrelled with your benefactress . . . it's time to put an end to all this. When I'm gone, everything will, I hope, settle down again and go back to what it was . . . Turning the heads of rich women and young girls is not the kind of thing I do . . . You'll forget me, and perhaps in time you'll wonder how all this could have happened . . . It seems astonishing to me even now . . . I don't want to deceive you, Vera Aleksandrovna: I'm scared, I'm terrified of staying here . . . I couldn't hold myself responsible for anything . . . I'm not used to this kind of thing, you know. I feel uncomfortable . . . I can't get rid of the feeling that everyone is looking at me . . . In fact, it wouldn't be possible for me . . . now . . . with you both . . .

VERA: Oh, don't worry yourself on my account, I won't be here much longer.

BELYAEV: What do you mean?

VERA: That's my secret. But I shan't be in your way, I can assure you.

BELYAEV: There now, you see, how can I possibly not go away? You can see for yourself. It's as if I'd brought a plague into this house: everyone is running away . . . it's better that I alone should disappear, while there's still time. I've just had a long conversation with Mr Rakitin . . . you can't imagine how bitter he was . . . He made fun of my new coat, and I deserved it . . . he is right. Yes, I must go. Believe me, Vera Aleksandrovna, I simply can't wait for the moment when I shall be rattling along in the cart on the high road . . . I'm suffocating here, I want to be out where I can breathe. I can't begin to tell you how miserable, and yet how light-hearted I feel, like a man setting off on a long journey overseas: he's sad at leaving his friends, he is frightened even, but the sound of the waves is so gay, and the wind blows so fresh in his face – it all sets his blood racing in his veins, no matter how heavy his heart . . . Yes, I'm definitely going. I shall go back to Moscow, to my friends, I'll start working . . .

VERA: So you do love her, Aleksei Nikolaich; you love her, and yet you're going away.

BELYAEV: Don't go on, Vera Aleksandrovna – what's the use? Don't you see that it's all over and done with? All of it. It flared up, and then it died like a spark. Let's part friends. It's time. I've come to my senses. Goodbye, may you be well and happy, we'll see each other again one day . . . I'll never forget you, Vera Aleksandrovna . . . I've grown very fond of you, believe me. *Presses her hand, and adds hurriedly.* Would you give this note to Natalya Petrovna for me?

VERA *looking at him in embarrassment:* Note?

BELYAEV: Yes . . . I can't say goodbye to her.

VERA: But are you going now?

BELYAEV: Yes, this minute . . . I haven't told anyone . . . except Mikhailo Aleksandrych. He's in favour of my going. I shall walk as far as Petrovskoye. I'll wait there for Mikhailo Aleksandrych and then we'll drive to town together. I'll write to you from there. My things will be sent on. You see, it's all arranged . . . By the way you can read the note. It's only two words.

VERA *taking the note from him:* Are you really going?

BELYAEV: Yes, yes . . . Give her this note and tell her . . . No, don't tell her anything. What is the point? *Listening.* Someone's coming . . . Goodbye. *Rushes to the door, stops for a moment in the doorway, and then runs off. Vera remains with the note in her hand. Natalya Petrovna enters from the hall.*

NATALYA PETROVNA *going up to Vera:* Verochka. *Looks at her, and stops.*

What's the matter? *Vera silently holds out the note.* A note? From whom?

VERA *in a dead voice:* Read it.

NATALYA PETROVNA: You frighten me. *Reads the note silently and suddenly presses both her hands to her face and collapses into an armchair. Long silence.*

VERA *going up to her:* Natalya Petrovna . . .

NATALYA PETROVNA *not taking her hands from her face:* He's going away! . . . he wouldn't even say goodbye to me . . . Oh! To you, at least, he said goodbye!

VERA *sadly:* He didn't love me . . .

NATALYA PETROVNA *takes her hands from her face and gets up:* But he had no right to go away like that . . . I want . . . he can't do this . . . who gave him permission to break off so stupidly . . . this really is contempt . . . I . . . How does he know that I should never have had the courage . . . *Sinks into the armchair.* Oh God, God! . . .

VERA: Natalya Petrovna, you told me yourself just now that he must go . . . don't you remember?

NATALYA PETROVNA: He's going . . . now you're pleased . . . that makes us even, doesn't it? *Her voice breaks.*

VERA: Natalya Petrovna, you said to me a moment ago . . . these were your very words: 'rather than torment each other, hadn't we better both think how we can get out of this situation, how we can save ourselves' . . . well, we're safe now.

NATALYA PETROVNA *moves away from her with something approaching hatred:* Oh!

VERA: I understand you, Natalya Petrovna . . . don't let it worry you . . . I shall not be a burden to you much longer . . . We cannot live together.

NATALYA PETROVNA *wants to hold out her hand, but lets it fall on her knee:* Why do you say that, Verochka . . . do you intend to leave me too? Yes, you are right, we are quite safe now. It's all over . . . it's all in order again . . .

VERA *coldly:* You've nothing to worry about, Natalya Petrovna. *Looks at her silently. Islayev comes from the study.*

ISLAYEV *looking for some time at Natalya Petrovna, in a low voice to Vera:* Does she know that he's going?

VERA *surprised:* Yes . . . she knows.

ISLAYEV *to himself:* Why did he leave in such a hurry? . . . *Aloud.*

Natasha . . . *Takes her by the hand. She lifts her head.* It's me, Natasha. *She tries to smile.* You're not well, my love? I think you really should lie down . . .

NATALYA PETROVNA: I'm quite well, Arkadi . . . it's nothing.

ISLAYEV: But you're so pale . . . Listen to me, you really should rest a little.

NATALYA PETROVNA: Yes, perhaps I should. *She tries to get up, but cannot.*

ISLAYEV *helping her:* You see? . . . *She leans on his arm.* Would you like me to come with you?

NATALYA PETROVNA: Oh no! I'm not as weak as all that! Let's go, Vera. *Moves towards the study, Rakitin comes out of the hall: Natalya Petrovna stops.*

RAKITIN: I've come, Natalya Petrovna . . .

ISLAYEV *interrupting:* Ah, Michel! come here! *Takes him aside and speaks to him in a low voice, with irritation.* Why did you have to tell her all this now? Surely I asked you not to — why all this hurry . . . I found her here in an awful state.

RAKITIN *with amazement:* I don't understand you.

ISLAYEV: You told Natasha that you were going away.

RAKITIN: You think *that's* what has upset her?

ISLAYEV: Shhh — she's looking at us. *Aloud.* Aren't you going to your room, Natasha?

NATALYA PETROVNA: Yes . . . I'm going . . .

RAKITIN: Goodbye, Natalya Petrovna! *Natalya Petrovna puts her hand on the door knob, and does not reply.*

ISLAYEV *putting his hand on Rakitin's shoulder:* You know, Natasha, he's one of the very best . . .

NATALYA PETROVNA *in a sudden outburst:* Yes — I know that he's a marvellous man — you are all marvellous people . . . All of you, all . . . Yet . . . *Suddenly covers her face with her hands, pushes the door open with her knee and quickly exits; Vera follows her. Islayev sits down in silence at the table and leans on his elbows.*

RAKITIN *looks at Islayev for a time, shrugs his shoulders with a bitter smile:* And where does this leave me? I'm in a fine position, I must say! Positively refreshing, one might say. And what a farewell after four years of love! Good! Excellent! Serve the old chatterbox right. Anyway, it's all for the best, thank heaven. It was time to put an end to these unhealthy, consumptive relationships. *Aloud, to Islayev.* Well, Arkadi, fare you well.

ISLAYEV *lifts his head. He has tears in his eyes:* Goodbye, old friend . . . Oh lord . . . it's not easy, no, not at all. I didn't expect it, my boy. It's been like a bolt from the blue. It'll all come right in the end, I suppose.[1] All the same . . . thank you, thank you – you are – a real friend!

RAKITIN *to himself, through clenched teeth:* This is too much. *Abruptly.* Goodbye. *Wants to go to the hall. Shpigelsky runs in towards him.*

SHPIGELSKY: What is it? I was told that Natalya Petrovna was ill . . .

ISLAYEV *getting up:* Who told you?

SHPIGELSKY: The girl . . . the housemaid . . .

ISLAYEV: No. It's nothing, Doctor. I think it's better not to disturb Natasha at the moment . . .

SHPIGELSKY: Ah well, splendid! *To Rakitin.* I am told that you are going into town?

RAKITIN: Yes: on business.

SHPIGELSKY: Ah, business! . . . *At this moment, Anna Semyonovna, Lizaveta Bogdanovna, Kolya and Schaaf all rush in together from the hall.*

ANNA SEMYONOVNA: What is it? What's the matter? Is something the matter with Natasha?

KOLYA: What's wrong with Mama? What is it?

ISLAYEV: Nothing's wrong . . . I saw her a minute ago . . . what's the matter with all of you?

ANNA SEMYONOVNA: Oh for goodness sake, Arkasha, we were told that Natasha was taken ill . . .

ISLAYEV: And you believed it . . .?

ANNA SEMYONOVNA: Why are you so cross, Arkasha? It's quite natural for us to be concerned.

ISLAYEV: Yes, of course . . . of course . . .

RAKITIN: However, it's time I went.

ANNA SEMYONOVNA: You're going away?

RAKITIN: Yes . . . I am.

ANNA SEMYONOVNA *speaking to herself:* Ah, now I understand.

KOLYA *to Islayev:* Papa . . .

ISLAYEV: What is it?

1 The Russian proverb is 'If the corn is ground, it'll turn to flour'.

KOLYA: Why did Aleksei Nikolaich go away?

ISLAYEV: Where has he gone?

KOLYA: I don't know . . . he kissed me, put on his cap and went out . . . It's time for my Russian lesson now.

ISLAYEV: Oh, I expect he'll be back in a moment . . . still, I'll send someone to find him.

RAKITIN *in a low voice:* Don't send for him, Arkadi, he is not coming back.

Anna Semyonovna is trying to overhear; Shpigelsky is talking in whispers to Lizaveta Bogdanovna.

ISLAYEV: What does this mean?

RAKITIN: He's going away too.

ISLAYEV: Going . . . where?

RAKITIN: To Moscow.

ISLAYEV: What do you mean, to Moscow! Has everyone gone mad today? What's going on?

RAKITIN *lowering his head:* Between ourselves . . . Verochka has fallen in love with him . . . Well, as a man of honour, he decided to leave.

Islayev flings up his arms and sinks into an armchair.

RAKITIN: You understand now, why . . .

ISLAYEV *leaping up:* Understand? I don't understand anything. My head's going round. What am I supposed to understand? Everybody is flying off in different directions, like a lot of partridges, and all because they are honourable people . . . all of them at once, all on the same day . . .

ANNA SEMYONOVNA *approaching from the side:* What is this? Mr Belyaev, you say . . .

ISLAYEV *shouting hysterically:* Nothing, Mama, nothing! Mr Schaaf, would you mind giving Kolya his lesson instead of Mr Belyaev? Could you please take him away?

SCHAAF: Yes, sir . . . *Takes Kolya by the hand.*

KOLYA: But, Papa . . .

ISLAYEV *shouting:* Go on, off you go! *Schaaf leads Kolya away.* Now, Rakitin, I'll see you off . . . I'll tell them to saddle a horse; I'll wait for you at the weir . . . And you, Mama, for God's sake don't

disturb Natasha, not now – nor you, Doctor, either . . . Matvei
. . . Matvei! *Goes out hurriedly.*

Anna Semyonovna sits down in sad, dignified fashion. Lizaveta Bogdanovna
places herself behind her. Anna Semyonovna lifts her eyes to heaven, as if to detach
herself completely from everything that is going on around her.

SHPIGELSKY *slyly and furtively to Rakitin:* Well, Mikhailo Aleksandrych, might I have the honour of taking you to the high road in my new troika?

RAKITIN: Oh . . . so you've got your horses already, have you?

SHPIGELSKY *modestly:* I've discussed things with Vera Aleksandrovna . . . So would you allow me?

RAKITIN: Why, thank you, yes! *Bows to Anna Semyonovna.* Anna Semyonovna, I have the honour . . .

ANNA SEMYONOVNA *does not rise; majestically:* Goodbye, Mikhailo Aleksandrych . . . may I wish you a happy journey . . .

RAKITIN: Thank you kindly. Lizaveta Bogdanovna . . . *Bows to her, she curtsies in reply. He goes into the hall.*

SHPIGELSKY *going up to kiss Anna Semyonovna's hand:* Goodbye, dear lady.

ANNA SEMYONOVNA *less majestically, but still sternly:* Oh, Doctor, you are going too?

SHPIGELSKY: Yes, ma'am . . . some of my patients, you know, are none too well. Besides, you know my presence isn't needed here. *Bows all round, with a sly look at Lizaveta Bogdanovna, who replies with a smile.* Goodbye . . . *Hurries off after Rakitin.*

ANNA SEMYONOVNA *lets him leave the room, crosses her arms and slowly turns to Lizaveta Bogdanovna:* What do you make of it all, my dear, eh?

LIZAVETA BOGDANOVNA *with a sigh:* I don't know, ma'am, what to say.

ANNA SEMYONOVNA: Have you heard? Belyaev is also going.

LIZAVETA BOGDANOVNA *sighs again:* Oh, Anna Semyonovna, I may not be staying here myself much longer . . . I'm going too.

Anna Semyonovna stares at her with indescribable amazement – Lizaveta Bogda-
novna stands before her without raising her eyes.

END

APPENDIX

THE CENSORSHIP OF THE TEXT

The first published version of *A Month in the Country* appeared in 1855, in the January issue of *The Contemporary* (*Sovremennik*), edited by the poet Nekrasov, with numerous deletions and substitutions demanded by the government censors. In the following year Nekrasov began to plan the reissue, in book form, of some of the more significant articles which had appeared in his journal, including some of Turgenev's plays. In connection with this, he instructed one of his assistant editors, D. Ya. Kolbasin, a fervent admirer of the novelist and one of his regular correspondents during the 1850s and early sixties, to supply him with a list of the excisions by the censors, to be (presumably) included, perhaps in a toned-down form, in the reprinted version. Kolbasin did so, and it is this list which is translated here, the censored words being printed in italics. Kolbasin's relevant letter, with the list of excisions, was published for the first time, so far as I know, in *Turgenev i krug 'Sovremennika'* (*Turgenev and the Circle of 'The Contemporary'*), ed. N. V. Izmailov, Akademia, Moscow-Leningrad, 1930, pp. 255–61, with useful notes by the editors of this correspondence (Ye. P. Naselenko and M. N. Motovilova), pp. 263–6.

ACT ONE
PAGE 23

l.1   'Thin, good figure, *long hair*, cheerful-looking, . . .'

l.2   'he's rather awkward, *not very soigné* . . .'

PAGE 28

l.15   Instead of 'he dances' the original had '*he manages to snatch*'.

l.16   Instead of 'rolls his eyes . . . unhappy I am', the original had '*says, from under his moustachios and through his nose, "Forget me not, the hour of parting strikes"*.'

ACT TWO
PAGE 41

l.26   '. . . the long-nosed stork. *Devil take him! To hell with him.*'

l.16 'the *shameful* pangs of . . .'

ACT THREE
l.29 '. . . There's only one thing surprises me – why do you keep going on about it so? *What is this Bolshintsov to you – a relation, is he?*

SHPIGELSKY: *Relation? I wouldn't lift a finger for a relation. I have an aunt in town, a cousin, rather – stands on the bridge selling buns – I've never given her anything in my life except an old waistcoat to make gloves out of.*

RAKITIN: *In that case, why are you trying so hard?*'

l.28 Instead of 'you were someone else.' the original had '*you were transfigured.*'

l.35 '. . . but young people are right, *do not marry anyone except for love . . .*'

l.36 'no, I didn't like him. *He moves his moustaches up to his nose in a funny sort of way, and looks at them.*'

ACT FOUR
l.20 Instead of 'I am not well-born', the original had '*I am a child of nature, in other words – a child of an unknown man's love*'

l.10 Instead of 'strangers' the original had '*the gentry*'.

l.12 Instead of 'these strangers' the original had '*these gentlefolk*'

l.14 'these very people, you know . . . *I praise them in such fashion that I wonder they don't take offence; it's as if every one of them were a model landowner, a pillar of the state, marvellously intelligent, a most wonderful husband, a father of unbelievable perfection, and, in addition to all this, a personal benefactor . . . naturally I say all this to their faces, otherwise why should I put myself to all this bother? . . . And what do you think? – each one listens to me with all his ears and doesn't notice that I am praising only him, and say the most*

awful things about all the others. (*After a silence*) . . . However, I
don't deceive' etc.

PAGE 90

l.1 'one of those *pig-headed* backwoodsmen – *who only stopped
neighing not so long ago,* while we were all . . .'

l.8 'how my life has turned out; *it's all my damnable poverty, yes,
and my birth too. I haven't much talent* . . .'

l.13 'need a better doctor; *they're pretty tough, there's no need to
think about them;* I'm good enough . . .'

l.19 'do what you like. *I don't suppose we shall have children, and
I see no reason for wanting them* . . . However, *if this disaster
does happen to us, I advise you to keep them away from me as
far as possible; I can't bear all that squealing.* There is, of
course . . .

PAGE 91

l.5 'real hopeless poverty is like . . . *You didn't run about barefoot in the streets, didn't shiver with cold and hide your frozen
hands in the sleeves of your wretched little shirt, your mother
– actually, the kindest of women – didn't go about in a
soldier's coat which some friend left her to remember him by
. . . ; you didn't wait hungrily for her return, like a starving
little wolf . . . you . . . but why go on! And then when, owing
to the kindness of a benefactor, whom, you will easily understand why, I hope to go on hating for the rest of my days, I got
to Moscow . . . entered the university* . . . However, I'll tell
you'

PAGE 93

l.1 'And his singing! *Just like a doctor.* Aleksei Nikolaich
may . . .'

ACT FIVE

PAGE 112

l.4 'rend the heart into little pieces . . . *And that's nothing* . . .
*Suffering? Man is created for this; and his whole life, point-
lessly wasted, spent utterly, worn out* . . . *that is what's so
terrible!* Just wait, you'll . . .'

l.8 '. . . kind of peace, *when you've lost the pride of strength and
the freshness of independence, you will begin to envy, envy*

painfully, any man who is *simple*, light-hearted and free . . .
You wait!'

l.15 'one has to be careful. *Believe me, Aleksei Nikolaich, only the
ordinary is natural and healthy; only the utterly commonplace . . . and I say this without any bitterness, I say it with
complete and deep conviction . . . only the commonplace is
worthy of respect, and woe unto him who dares break the
sacred laws of everyday life.*'

The censor had originally required the excision of almost the
whole of this speech (from l.1, 'every kind of love . . .'), but
it was reincorporated, virtually as it now stands, in the published text of 1869.

l.24 Instead of 'women' (twice), the original had 'ladies'.

l.31 'piece of good advice. *The thing is this, Aleksei Nikolaich: if
ever you happen to notice that a woman has suddenly begun
to feel something for you, don't lose time, seize the opportunity, seize it with both hands, to hell with fine feelings;
women's love is like a brook in spring: one day it rushes,
excited and turbid, rising to the gulley's edges, the next day it
scarcely moves, a thin, fresh little trickle along the dried up
bed of the stream. Stops and gives an impatient wave of the hand.* Oh,
but really, it's hardly for me . . .'

PAGE 118

l.4 Instead of 'I must go', the original text had '*Freedom before
everything*'.

PAGE 121

l.21 ANNA SEMYONOVNA: *Oh God in heaven, Lord of my
being*, what is it?

A further passage [Act One, p. 33, lines 34–37, 'our relationship' to
'that's why'], omitted in the 1855 edition, was restored in 1869.
The editors of the complete Soviet edition of 1962 think it probable
that this, too, had been cut by the censor.[1]

1 I. S. Turgenev, *Sochineniya*, t.3, Moscow, 1962, pp. 58, 334, 418.